DECEPTION

A CONNOR MAXWELL MYSTERY

TIMOTHY GLASS

Platinum Paw Press

CONTENTS

DECEPTION

A CONNOR MAXWELL MYSTERY

Deception

Written by Timothy Glass

Copyright (C) 2019

Cover art by Timothy Glass

Library of Congress Control Number 2019907426

Platinum Paw Press

ISBN number 978-1-7331972-0-5

DEDICATION

To the memory of Karen Perry, my beloved sister-in-law, you were and still are my hero for your battle with cancer. Your smile was the light of our lives. Fly with the wings of angels. For those who knew you I know your life will never be forgotten and you deserved so much better.

ACKNOWLEDGMENTS

As always, thank you to my wife; you are my compass to keep me on my true north.

To my wonderful fans who support my craft.

To my brothers in blue, Ronald S., Pete R., and Charlie W. who lost their lives in the line of duty.

Once again, to all the first responders who put a uniform on with no promise of coming home at the end of your shifts. You are the true heroes spending countless hours putting your lives on the line and in many situations, it is a thankless job.

QUOTE

"It is the man's own mind, not his enemy or foe, that
lures him to evil ways."
Buddha

Sundae

CHAPTER 1

The pearl-white BMW with dark-tinted windows traveled slowly around the parking lot. The lone male driver stopped as a well-dressed couple came out of the restaurant, carrying a white Styrofoam box. The man leaned over and kissed the woman, then opened her car door.

Turning the BMW, the driver went through the parking lot again and looked at his watch. In his head, he replayed their conversation from the day before, when he had nonchalantly asked her what hours she worked. He clearly remembered her saying that she started work at 6:00 a.m. and got off at 3:00 p.m. It was now already 3:30. What was taking her so long? He gripped the steering wheel harder as he wondered whether she ever had to cover someone else's shift.

The door to the restaurant opened and she walked out. He quickly pulled into a parking slot and waited. Tapping on the steering wheel, he nervously watched as her Chevy Blazer backed out of her parking spot. Once the backup lights were off, he threw the BMW into reverse. Staying a safe distance from her car, he followed her, turn by turn. They became separated at the traffic light at Orange Grove and Kings Road.

"Come on, come on!" he yelled at the light.

Once it turned green, he sped up and finally caught a glimpse of the Blazer's taillights. He resumed following the young woman. Her brake lights came on as she slowed her SUV to navigate the Chevy into the turn, then pulled into the driveway of her home at 1313 K Falls Road. It was one in a row of newer townhomes.

He pulled the BMW to the curb and watched her exit the SUV, then walk up the sidewalk and unlock the front door.

That was all he needed for now. Tomorrow would be the big day. As he pulled away from the curb, he looked around. "Good. No one around," said the man as he pulled off his blonde wig and tossed it into the backseat. *The hunter and the prey*, he thought to himself and smiled.

The following morning, the alarm woke him at 5:00 a.m. He quickly showered. Before leaving the hotel room, he wiped away any trace of himself. Tossing his suitcases into the trunk, he chuckled to think that the hotel would be stiffed with one of the bogus credit cards he had used.

At 5:15, he pulled into an alleyway. With the keys still in the ignition, he wiped down the car and then abandoned it. He hoped someone would steal the Beamer. He walked to the rental car agency. Along with a fake ID, another stolen credit card, and the story of how he'd had to walk from the airport, bag and baggage in hand, he rented a nondescript sedan.

He pulled into traffic and drove toward the townhome at 1313 K Falls Road. Once there, he made sure not to park too close to the Chevy Blazer. He pulled all the way over to the line on the driver's side, leaving room between the rental car and her SUV so that his plan could work. Next, he wiped the car clean and then exited the rental car, leaving the doors unlocked.

The dawn sky was a hazy, grayish color. He looked at his watch; about twenty minutes until sunrise if his smartphone app was to be believed. He walked while taking in his surroundings, heading back toward the highway from which he'd come. Counting the tall shrubs as he walked, he made a mental note that there were exactly five. He turned right and was now on the opposite side from where he had parked and where another row of townhomes stood. Looking around this parking lot, he found it empty at this time of the morning. The shrubs divided the two sections of townhomes. *Maybe for privacy*, he thought. From the opposite side, he counted the shrubs.

"Five," he said to himself as he squeezed through the shrubs. "Perfect."

Looking around to make sure no one was watching, he quickly bent down and crawled beneath the Chevy Blazer. The asphalt was cold as he lay under her SUV. It was mid-October; the days were shorter and a chill was in the air. More importantly, the sun came up later, if at all.

He lay in wait on the asphalt under her Chevy Blazer. It was fifteen minutes before six. He heard a door open and close. Was it her? Hearing footsteps, he glanced out from under the car. He saw a pair of men's black dress shoes. Not her. His plan would work only if she left within the next few minutes, before more residents started leaving.

Suddenly he heard another door open, followed by soft footsteps nearing her SUV. There she was. He recognized her shoes. He'd been careful to observe her footwear each time he'd been in the restaurant.

His heart pounded and adrenaline coursed through his veins. He heard her keys fall from her hand just short of the back tire on the driver's side. He panicked. From her vantage point as she bent to retrieve her keys, would she be able to see him lying under the SUV? If so, his plan would be foiled. He lay perfectly still as he watched her hands reach for the keys. He heard the door locks click open as she unlocked the vehicle...

He had to make his move now. He stretched out

4

both of his large, muscular arms and grabbed her ankles. He pulled as hard as he could, knocking her off her feet. He heard the thud as she fell and then he quickly climbed out from under the SUV. She was stunned as he pounced on her and put the ether to her face. Her eyes rolled back. Looking around, he tossed her lifeless body into the backseat of her SUV. Next, he pulled his suitcases from the rental. Climbing into the backseat, he quickly pulled the duct tape from his bag and taped her mouth. He tightly wrapped her wrists behind her back and taped her ankles. Satisfied with his work, he grabbed her keys, jumped into the driver's seat, and pulled onto the street.

CHAPTER 2

The red truck screeched to a stop, its tires leaving two long, black skid marks behind them. The right front tire was up against the curb while the rear end was about four feet from the curb. Tanner Dolan, age twenty-five, jumped from the cab, leaving the driver's side door open. With his long legs, he quickly reached the sidewalk that cut a path down the center of the perfectly manicured yard.

The red brick two-story was one of about 200 homes in Lakewood Estates, an affluent neighborhood on the west side of Lakewood that boasted a country club, golf course, restaurant, tennis court, swimming pool, and walking trail.

Tanner rang the doorbell repeatedly and then banged his fists on the front door.

"Mr. and Mrs. Howell, open up! She didn't come home last night or this morning!" Tanner's voice cracked; he was now out of breath. "Open up!" He continued pounding on the door and ringing the bell.

The sun had just poked its lazy head over the surrounding mountains, spreading its golden light across the city of Lakewood below. The rapid knocking on the front door of the Howell home at 1512 Denton Drive continued.

Mr. Howell turned over in bed and looked at the nightstand clock, which displayed 5:45 a.m. He turned back to his wife, who had already gotten out of bed and pulled on her blue bathrobe.

"It's probably Amber. Maybe she forgot her house keys again," Mrs. Howell said.

"At this hour? Is this the day she comes over to do her laundry?" Mr. Howell grumbled.

By now his wife was three-quarters of the way down the hall and he knew she probably hadn't heard a word he'd just said. Mr. Howell shook his head and turned over. Pulling the covers up to his chin, he closed his eyes and hoped for at least another hour of sleep.

"Henry, come down here!" Mrs. Howell yelled from downstairs.

Mr. Howell opened one eye, then the other, and swung both legs out from under the bed covers.

"Now what?" Henry said under his breath.

Wearing only a pair of boxer shorts and a t-shirt, he grabbed his pants and a shirt he had laid on the dresser the night before. Rubbing the sleep from his eyes, he made his way downstairs, where he found Amber's boyfriend, Tanner Dolan, nervously pacing in their living room.

"She didn't come home last night. It's just not like her," Tanner said, looking from Mr. to Mrs. Howell.

"Maybe she stayed at a friend's house, " Mr. Howell suggested.

"No … she would have called to tell me," Tanner said, panic in his voice.

Mr. Howell watched Tanner pace back and forth. He shook his head and turned back to his wife with raised eyebrows.

"It's just not like her!" Tanner stopped in front of Mr. Howell.

Mr. Howell stepped around Tanner. He hated it when anyone invaded his personal space and got into his face. Henry walked over to the foyer table and picked up his phone.

"I'll call her cell phone."

"I've already done that, even called her work to see if maybe she took a double shift," Tanner said, throwing his arms outward in frustration to get his point across.

"Amber, this is Dad. Give us a call when you get this message," Mr. Howell said into the phone, then disconnected the call.

Next, Henry dialed Amber's work number using the speed dial on his phone.

"May I please speak to Allison…" He covered

the mouthpiece and looked over to his wife. "What's Allison's last name?"

"Walker … I think," Mrs. Howell said.

"Allison Walker," Mr. Howell said into the phone.

Several minutes later, he disconnected the call and sat down. "Her boss said she didn't show up for work yesterday."

"Tanner, was there a fight between you two?" Mrs. Howell asked.

Tanner stopped and turned back to Mrs. Howell.

"Nine-one-one, what's your emergency?" Sandy Curtis asked. Sandy was a seasoned police dispatcher who had been with the Lakewood Police Department for six years.

"My name is Henry Howell. Our daughter, Amber, didn't come home last night or this morning and she didn't show up for work yesterday. This just isn't like her."

Lakewood, like many cites, had experienced urban sprawl. New housing developments had begun dotting the Lakewood landscape like anthills on a Southwestern desert. Along with them came new families and not-so-familiar faces. At one time, everyone had known their neighbors and greeted them with a wave or a friendly "hello." Today, that seemed to be a thing of the past. Families were attracted to the weather in Lakewood. The summer months were warm, and children could frolic and play by the surrounding lakeshore. Families could boat, water ski, and fish. In the fall, the trees put on their displays of beautiful hues, including shades of red, yellow, and orange. During the winter, Lakewood got a little snow and the nearby mountains attracted skiers, snowboarders, and snowmobilers from all over the country.

Nonetheless, no city was immune to crime and Lakewood's crime stats were climbing despite the fact that both the Lakewood Police Department and the Natick County Sherriff's Department had increased the number of their officers.

Detective Kate Stroup stepped out of the shower wrapped in a large pink towel. She dried herself off. In the background, a George Winston CD played softly. As she buttoned her blouse, her dark brown eyes were drawn to the lesion on her chest. She brushed her shoulder length auburn hair. It had been over six months since she'd been shot and almost killed. The shooting had left a scar on both her body and her emotions. She had been cleared for duty after a lengthy hospital stay, physical therapy, and weekly visits to the department psychologist. She used this time off duty to build up her strength and clear her mind through her new hobby: paddle boarding. She had bookmarked a wetsuit online, which would allow her to extend her new hobby into the cooler months. Nonetheless, she had found herself home alone.

The honking of a horn brought her thoughts back to the present day, her first one back on the job. She quickly tucked her 9mm Glock into the pancake holster on her belt. Grabbing her badge, she ran outside. Parked in the driveway was a plain vanilla, as they called the unmarked cars at the police department. Behind the wheel sat her partners: Detective Connor Maxwell and his canine beagle companion, Sundae.

Connor watched Kate pull her front door closed. Her face was tanned, and her five-foot, four-inch-tall body was fit. He found himself remembering the kiss they had shared the previous year. Both of them knew all too well the departmental policy of not dating one's partner. It didn't matter. They hadn't gone beyond the kiss.

Kate opened the police unit door and looked at Connor. She thought he looked tired, but she had been following the news and knew he was probably working endless hours on the Howell case. Kate smiled at Connor as she sat in the passenger seat.

Connor gave her a boyish grin and brushed a lock of unruly brown hair from his forehead.

Connor was a hard worker, but loved to hike and camp. She thought by the look on his face that he had not been able to get away for any down time. To Kate, Connor was a no-nonsense man. He usually dressed in Wrangler jeans, a dress shirt, a sport coat and his boots that he called his Okie Airs. Needless to say, he caught the eye of most women including Kate. She remembered waking up in the hospital with Connor asleep in a chair next to her bed and Sundae curled up on the bed beside her.

"Any word on the Howell case?" Kate asked as she settled in. "I saw the news last night on the TV."

"Boyfriend is coming in today at 9:00 for another interview," Connor said as he pulled the police unit back out onto the street. "Search teams have turned up nothing and it's been almost twenty-four hours since it was reported."

"Think the boyfriend had something to do with it?" Kate asked.

"Not sure what to think at this point."

Connor made a right turn onto Main Street. Kate looked into the backseat, where Sundae was looking out the window.

"How about you, Sundae … got any ideas?"

Sundae looked at Kate then back out the window.

The search teams walked shoulder to shoulder through the wooded areas in and around Lakewood. The smell of coffee wafted through the morning air, mixed with the scent of pine trees. A table with coffee and snacks for the volunteers and professional searchers was set up next to a makeshift headquarters for the police and sheriff's departments. In town, fliers with Amber's photo were already being hung on signposts, street lamps, and anywhere else they could be placed.

Mr. Howell stood at the intersection of Main and 10th Streets. As the traffic light turned red, he stepped off the median carrying a stack of fliers and walked toward the first car.

"My daughter is missing. Can you please tell me if you've seen her?" he asked the driver, then handed him a flyer.

Mr. Howell tried to have faith that Amber would come back home or call. The seconds since she'd left had turned into hours. Mr. Howell helped hang up posters while his wife stayed home. No calls had been made to the house, where the police had set up special equipment to capture any incoming calls with a demand for money. The fact that there were no demands meant that there were no leads.

Mr. Howell looked at his watch. They were nearing the twenty-four-hour mark of Amber's disappearance. He had to get back home, where he, his wife, and Tanner would be holding a press conference to plead for Amber's safe return.

A set of microphones had been placed at a small podium. Behind them, the police chief of Lakewood provided Amber's physical description and a phone number for anyone who knew anything about her whereabouts.

"Can you tell us if you have any leads at this time?" called out Candy Martin, a news reporter with one of the local TV stations.

"This is an ongoing investigation and we cannot comment on that at this time."

CHAPTER 3

When Connor and Kate entered the restaurant, a friendly hostess greeted them. "Welcome to the Lakota," she said with a pleasant smile.

Connor reached for his ID. "My name is Detective Maxwell, and this is my partner, Detective Stroup. We would like to speak to the manager if we could."

The Lakota had changed hands several times since its grand opening in the 1970s. It had been built aside a mountain that overlooked Lakewood's largest lake, Lake Lakota. The interior was breathtaking, as one wall was the actual mountain itself, with a small waterfall that drained into a pond. The beautifully set tables featured wine-colored tablecloths, each topped with a shorter white cloth. Some tables were close to the pond while others were spread out toward the glass walls overlooking Lake Lakota. To say the inside was picturesque would be an understatement. The tranquil sound of the waterfall made it even more pleasant. The restaurant served a great breakfast, lunch, and dinner menu, and for ten years in a row, *Lakewood Magazine* had named it one of the city's top restaurants. Amber Howell had been a waitress there for the last few years.

"Follow me," said the hostess as she escorted them to a table. "I'll let her know you're here."

Once they were seated, the hostess motioned to a waitress to bring them water and coffee on the house.

"She didn't ask us why we're here," Kate commented, looking at Connor.

"Lakewood has grown, but I'm sure everyone has seen the news."

"You're right," Kate said.

Two large coffee cups were set down with a pot of fresh coffee between them, along with fresh water and glasses.

"If I can bring you anything else, please let me know."

Kate and Connor thanked the waitress as a woman, fortyish, with short, styled hair and large blue eyes walked over to their table. She extended her hand to both Connor and Kate as she introduced herself, then took her seat.

"I'm Madison Santos, the general manager here at the Lakota. How may I help?"

"Ms. Santos, thank you for seeing us on such short notice. As I'm sure you know, Amber is still missing," Connor said. "We're wondering: When was the last time you saw Amber Howell?"

"It was Tuesday. She worked the day shift, her usual eight hours and left. Wait … Come to think of it, her supervisor asked her to stay an extra thirty minutes on Tuesday. Her relief came in late that day. She was supposed to work Wednesday but didn't show up for her shift," Santos said.

"You mentioned her supervisor. What did you say her name was?" Kate asked.

"I'm sorry, her name is Allison Walker," Ms. Santos said. She watched Kate write down the name.

"Is Allison here today?" Connor asked.

"No, it's her day off. She's one of the volunteers searching for Amber now. Our restaurant has taken food and coffee to the search site," Ms. Santos replied.

"That was nice of your restaurant to do that," Kate said.

"Amber is well-liked here. It's the least we can do. I've put in a request with the manager to provide a reward as well. I'm still waiting for a reply," Ms. Santos said.

"Has Amber ever done this before? I mean, missed work without calling in?" asked Connor.

"No, never," Ms. Santos replied.

"Did she have any problems here at work or

with another employee, or even a customer?" Connor asked.

"Detectives, Amber got along with everyone she worked with here. In my ten years here, we've had a lot of churn, if you know what I mean. Wait staff comes and goes. It's the same with the backroom staff. But Amber has been with us for several years. I've never heard anyone complain about her."

"Any customers of late who may have had an issue with her?"

As the manager talked, Kate wrote down everything in a small notebook she carried in her pocket.

"Not that I'm aware of. Let me get Maggie; they usually work together. Maybe she can be of help. Would that be okay?"

"Of course," Connor said.

The manager stood and motioned for a young woman to come over. The waitress was a small brunette whose hair was pulled back in a ponytail. She smiled and approached the table.

"Maggie, this is Detective Maxwell and Detective Stroup of the Lakewood Police Department. I told them you and Amber usually work the day shift together."

Connor stood. He shook Maggie's hand and gave both his and Kate's business cards to her.

Maggie looked to be in her mid-twenties. She took her seat across from the two detectives, quickly placing Kate's card beneath Connor's.

Kate watched closely as Maggie looked Connor over. She silently reassured herself that she and Connor were merely partners and that her close observation of Maggie was nothing more than an attempt to read her body language.

"Maggie, we were wondering if you have any knowledge of anyone with whom Amber could have had problems, either here at work or outside of work," Kate said.

Maggie looked down at the table, playing with the two business cards, then tapping her right hand on the table in thought. From Kate's vantage point, she could see a small tattoo on the inside of Maggie's forearm: a puppy paw with a heart around it.

"Amber got along with most everyone here," Maggie said, looking only at Connor.

"Did she ever mention her home life with Tanner to you?" Connor asked.

"Sure, but as far as I know, they were good. I guess what I'm saying is that she never complained about the dude. Why? Do you think Tanner had something to do with this?" Maggie asked.

"At this time, we're looking into anyone, past or present, whom Maggie was involved with. That's all," Connor said.

Connor looked around the room, collecting his thoughts.

"Maggie, did Amber ever mention someone else, like an ex-boyfriend, to you?"

"She was dating…" Maggie stopped mid-sentence and looked over at her manager. "Do you remember that guy's name … you know, the one before Tanner? Remember, he had all those tattoos up his arms and on his neck?"

Madison Santos thought for a moment. "I remember him coming in to pick her up but I don't remember his name. I'm sorry."

Kate quickly wrote down the description of the ex-boyfriend.

"Any idea why they broke up?"

"Amber found out he was going out with another woman, so she dumped him."

Kate watched Maggie play with the two business cards in her hands.

"Do either of you know anyone else she dated?" Connor asked.

Both Madison Santos and Maggie shook their heads no.

"Did Amber ever have any issues with a customer here?" Kate asked.

"Not that I recall," Madison Santos said and Maggie shook her head no.

Connor and Kate stood.

"If you think of anything, anything at all, please give us a call," Connor said.

Kate noticed Maggie had left her business card on the table.

"We'll do that. Detectives, please find her," Madison said.

Back at the police unit, Connor opened the car's trunk. From a brown paper bag that Tanner had given to him, Connor removed a pink blouse belonging to Amber. He held the blouse to Sundae's nose and gave her the command to search the exterior of the Lakota restaurant and around the lake. The white tip of Sundae's tail was off and running as she trotted with her nose to the ground, tracking back and forth on a trail leading toward the lake.

Connor and Kate followed, watching Sundae as she tracked completely around the lake.

When Sundae returned to Connor's side, it was clear to both detectives that she hadn't picked up anything during her search.

As Connor pulled the unmarked car out of the driveway, the police radio broke through the silence in the car.

"15," said Sandy Curtis, the police dispatcher.

"15, go ahead," Connor replied.

"We just had a report of one of Amber Howell's credit cards being used. I knew you were 10-6 at the Lakota and dispatched Detectives Barton and Harris to check it out."

"10-4. Ask them to find out whether the place has video that would show the time stamp on the charge, if they haven't already."

"10-4, 15."

CHAPTER 4

B ob Barton and Grant Harris sat inside the back office of The Gold and Silver Shop just off Hanson Street in downtown Lakewood. Fritz Otto, the manager of The Gold and Silver Shop, was a short, rotund man who appeared to be in his early sixties. The gold and silver business must have been going well, as he was dressed in what looked like a dark blue Armani suit. He wore a Rolex watch on his wrist. Fritz sat behind his equally expensive desk. Detective Harris looked down and tried to smooth out the wrinkles in his JC Penney sports coat.

The charge was for three 100-ounce gold bars. Across his desk, the manager passed a copy of the receipt along with a copy of the photo ID. The clerk who made the sale had copied the documents.

"Does your store always make copies of customers' IDs?" asked Detective Barton.

"Yes, it's policy."

Barton detected a slight accent from Fritz but couldn't figure out where it was from. Both detectives studied the purchase paperwork that the manager had handed them. Bob pointed to the card slip, noting that Amber's charge card said "A. Howell" while the photo ID said "Albert Howell." Whoever Albert Howell was, he definitely wasn't Amber, though her card company had approved the charge.

The Lakewood PD had asked the Howells not to cancel Amber's credit cards. Connor had called the card company's fraud department and explained that Amber was missing, along with her purse and SUV. The police had a theory that they might be able to trace any purchases and locations where the cards were used. In theory, this should have worked. With the cards flagged, the fraud department should have contacted the Lakewood Police Department ASAP. However, something had gone terribly wrong and the charge had been cleared.

The Xerox copy of the photo on the ID was grainy. Grant passed the copy of the ID to Bob.

"Bad copy machine?" Bob looked up at the manager.

"No. I asked the clerk on duty why the photo was so distorted."

"And?" Detective Barton asked.

"This 'Albert Howell' guy had told the clerk that there's a place in the Lakewood Mall that puts a protective film over IDs. He told the clerk he did this because he didn't want his ID scuffed."

Didn't want his ID scuffed, Bob thought to himself and shook his head.

"This is no protective film. This is more like the protective film on license plates which renders the plate numbers unreadable by red-light cameras," Bob said as he handed the copy back to Grant, who also noticed how distorted the picture looked. Even the most pronounced facial features weren't clear.

"May we get a copy of all this paperwork to take back to the police department?" Detective Grant asked.

"Of course," the manager replied and left the room.

"Connor isn't going to be happy with this," Bob said to Grant as Fritz returned with a copy for each of them.

"Can you tell me if these 100-ounce gold bars are traceable?" Detective Barton asked.

"Many large companies, such as Johnson and Matthey, do have serial numbers on their bullion. During the minting of precious metals, a serial number can be embossed into the bar. Many investors believe a numbered bar is worth more. However, this customer chose three bars that had nothing but the 100 oz. 999.9 on the bar," the manager explained

"If I understand you correctly, there are no

distinguishing marks of any kind on these bars and they're untraceable?" asked Detective Barton.

"That's correct. He can take these bars to a hock shop or another gold and silver exchange dealer and get the current hourly rate, less the broker's commission," said the shop owner as he clicked away on his computer keyboard. He then turned his monitor toward the two detectives.

"As you can see, as of this hour, gold is trading for $1,234 an ounce. When the man purchased the bars, gold was at $1,200. If he holds onto them, he stands to make even more," the manager said as he turned his monitor back.

"Given the fact that he paid with a stolen credit card and has in his possession a full profit and untradeable items, he knows what he's doing," Detective Harris countered.

"Do you have any video surveillance in your shop?" Detective Barton asked.

The manager looked down and nervously adjusted his desk blotter.

"We do. However, several minutes before he came in, our cameras went dark. That was the first thing I thought about after the fraud department finally contacted us asking if the person was still here. In looking at the poor quality of the photo ID, I knew the video would be of help to the police. When I pulled the video, I noticed it had gone dark."

"It went dark … like, very little light? What are you saying, Mr. Otto?" Detective Harris asked.

"Completely out. Nothing. Just black," said the manager. "It was like something was interfering with the reception on the cameras. We have nothing but a black screen."

CHAPTER 5

The Box, as the detectives at the Lakewood Police Department liked to call it, was a small room with drab walls and a two-by-four-foot metal table. The room also had two – or sometimes three – wooden chairs. On the long wall dividing the hallway from the Box was a large window. By design, the one-way glass allowed people in the hallway to see into the Box, while people inside the Box couldn't see out.

Tanner Dolan sat waiting for Detectives Maxwell and Stroup. Before entering, the two detectives stood in the hallway outside the Box, watching the young man for a few seconds. Kate pulled an extra chair into the room as Connor sat across from Tanner. Sundae sat next to Connor's feet.

"Tanner, this is my partner, Detective Kate Stroup. She was out the first day we talked, but she'll be working the case with me," Connor said as Kate shook Tanner's hand.

Kate noted that his hand wasn't sweaty like many people's hands were when they were nervous. She wrote that fact in her notepad.

"Tanner, have you thought of anything else about Amber's disappearance that might help us?" Connor asked.

"No, nothing." Tanner paused. "But we did find this." He reached into his faded jeans and pulled out a gold, heart-shaped pendant, then handed it to Connor.

Connor looked it over carefully, then handed the pendant to Kate.

"Where'd you find this?" Kate asked.

"Amber always parks in the same place. It's a little odd, but where we live, people are considerate and don't take another person's parking spot." Tanner's eye darted back and forth from Connor to Kate. "Anyway, the parking spot next to Amber's is Mr. Wallace's. The day after we reported Amber missing, Mr. Wallace came to our townhome and asked if this was Amber's. I told him yes; the heart was on a necklace I had given Amber for her birthday last year."

Tanner pulled out his wallet and quickly thumbed through the plastic picture dividers in it. Once he found the photo, he removed it and placed it on the table. Connor looked at the image of a brightly smiling Amber Howell. She was wearing the gold, heart-shaped necklace that Kate now held in her hand.

"Do you know for certain that Amber parked in her *place*, as you call it, that night?"

"She asked me to take her dad's books out to her SUV for her while she cooked dinner. It was parked in her spot."

"What exactly do you mean, *her father's books*?" Kate asked.

"He's a CPA and Amber makes extra money helping with the bookkeeping for her dad."

"Tanner, would you mind if we kept the heart? We'll send it to our CSI tech team and see if they can pull anything off it," Kate asked.

"It'll have my prints on it … and probably Mr. Wallace's," Tanner quickly responded.

"Understood," Kate said. "I'll just be a minute while I make a copy of this photo and we can give it back to you." Kate got up, leaving the necklace on the table, and left the room with the photo in hand.

"Tanner, once Detective Stroup returns, do you have time to show us where Amber always parks and maybe introduce us to Mr. Wallace?"

"Sure."

Tanner pulled his truck in a parking place across from the townhome he and Amber shared. Connor was aware that the CSI team had looked over the townhome and he assumed they had checked the parking lot as well. However, he wondered if they'd had any idea that the residents each had their own unmarked parking spot. Or had they simply missed it?

"Here." Tanner pointed to an empty parking place.

Next to that spot sat a large, black Dodge Ram truck. Connor looked at the Ram and then back to the empty parking place. He wondered if the residents who knew that Amber was missing were simply hoping she'd return and had left the spot empty out of respect.

"That's Mr. Wallace's truck. He must be home," Tanner said.

Connor took a brown paper bag from the trunk of his police unit. He opened the bag and let Sundae sniff Amber's blouse, then gave her a command to search. Sundae zigzagged through the parking lot, the white tip of her tail held high above her back. The tri-colored beagle had her nose to the ground. A few seconds later, she quickly sat next to Amber's parking spot and howled.

"Wow … she's good!" Tanner said, impressed with the thirteen-inch beagle's skills.

Connor gave Sundae the release command as he and Kate checked the bushes next to the parking spot. Between the bushes, toward the front of the parking spot, they found footprints in the soil.

"This could have been our perp," Connor said to Kate.

"I'll call our techs back out to cast the footprints."

"Tanner, are you absolutely sure that Amber wouldn't have just left on her own, for any reason whatsoever, and not wanted anyone to know where she was going?"

"Detective, you asked me that the first day we filed the missing person report. The answer is still no. It's not like Amber to not call … she always calls me several times a day to see how I'm doing. She also calls her mother," Tanner said as a door behind them opened and closed. A tall, silver-haired man walked toward them.

"That's Mr. Wallace." Tanner pointed toward the man.

"Great. I was just going to ask you which home he lived in so we could talk to him," Connor said.

As Connor walked toward Mr. Wallace, he gave Kate a look. Kate knew not to follow or to allow Tanner to follow Connor, so she engaged Tanner in conversation.

"Mr. Wallace, my name is Connor Maxwell and my partner over there is Detective Kate Stroup. May I have a few minutes of your time?" Connor asked.

"Of course. Should we go over there?" Mr. Wallace pointed to Kate and Tanner.

"No, actually, I'd rather not. Let's talk over

here." Connor took Mr. Wallace out of earshot of Tanner and Kate. "Tanner tells us that, in the parking lot somewhere, you found a gold heart pendant that belongs to Amber. Is that correct?"

"Yes. I must've missed it the other day, but yesterday morning when I got home from work, I saw it."

"Not the day before?" Connor questioned.

"No," Mr. Wallace said. "The other morning, a small, silver car with out-of-state plates was parked in my spot. I'm not sure if Tanner explained to you that we all have our own spots here. While they're unmarked, we know what spot belongs to townhome number four and so on."

Connor interrupted Mr. Wallace. "You're saying that a car you didn't recognize as one from the neighborhood was parked in your spot?"

"That's correct. Plus, it was parked half in my spot and half in the next spot, which belongs to Pete. He leaves for work really early in the morning. I work nights and come in at around 7:15 a.m."

"Do you remember the make, model, or license plate number, by any chance?"

"I wish I did. All I remember is it was a silver car and it had out-of-state plates. Honestly, I assumed it was someone visiting one of the neighbors here. When I left for work again at 11:00 that night, the car was gone."

Did you happen to see anyone move the car during the day?" Connor asked

"No, I'm sorry, I didn't."

"Mr. Wallace, just so I'm clear, where again was the heart pendant found?" Connor asked. He followed Mr. Wallace to the passenger's side of his truck.

Mr. Wallace bent down on his haunches. "About there." He pointed, and then looked back at Connor. "Oh, one thing I do remember is that the car had a rental sticker on the bumper."

"Would you mind coming down to the police department to make a formal statement?"

"Not at all," Mr. Wallace said.

CHAPTER 6

Connor paced in front of the whiteboard. A five-by-seven-inch photo of Amber was taped to the top left. From there, a line had been drawn down to another photo, that of Tanner Dolan, Amber's boyfriend. Below that was a photo of the parking lot. A red dry marker line marked Amber's parking spot.

The CSI team had carefully cast and photographed the shoe prints that cut through the bushes by Amber's empty parking spot. The whiteboard also included the photos of the cast that the CSI team had made, as well as a photo of the print in the soil. In red marker, next to the shoe photos, were the words "men's Nike size 10." The last photo was that of the gold pendant. To the other side of Amber's photo was a red box drawn with a question mark: no photo or name. Next to it were the words "ex-boyfriend with tats."

"What are we missing?" Connor asked, frustrated that they had nothing more on the case.

Kate placed the handset of her phone back on the cradle.

"That was the team at the Howell house. No one has called making a demand as of yet."

"What about the rental car business?" Connor asked.

"We have a pearl-white BMW that wasn't returned on time. It was found in an alley. They did say the person renting the car had given a fake ID and credit card."

"That doesn't match the description Mr. Wallace gave us of the small silver car," Connor said, rubbing his hand over his face, deep in thought. "Can you ask Barton and Harris to follow up on the BMW? Maybe there's a connection."

"By the way, the rental car business in town said they have more silver cars on their lots than any other color," Kate said as she looked down, reading from the notes on her desk.

"Anything on the tip hotline?"

"Oh, we have tips but so far, they've turned out to be nothing. This morning Sandy said a man called in and said that an alien space ship had been sighted in Lakewood and that aliens have her."

Connor laughed as he watched Kate reach instinctively toward her chest, rubbing the spot where she'd been shot.

"Still hurt?" Connor asked.

Kate looked up at Connor, surprised, not realizing she had been rubbing the scar on her chest. "They told me it's probably scar tissue; nothing to be worried about."

"Have you seen the big tipper lately?" Alison asked Maggie as the lunch crowd began to thin out and tables were cleared and reset at the Lakota restaurant.

"No, come to think of it, I haven't," Maggie said as she rushed past Alison, delivering a tray full of food, the aroma wafting after her.

"Probably a tourist … people come and go," Alison said under her breath as she walked back into the kitchen.

Suddenly, Maggie burst through the kitchen doors and tossed her serving tray onto a counter.

"What?" Alison looked at Maggie and then out into the dining room.

"That's it!" Maggie said.

"What's it … what's wrong?" Alison looked at Maggie, confused.

"Where is it?" Maggie said as she rushed over to the locker area.

"Maggie, I'm getting worried. Is something wrong?"

"I need to find his card," Maggie said, rooting through her messy locker, tossing items from one side to the other. "Damn … what was his name? Don? No, that doesn't sound right. Maybe John."

Maggie continued digging frantically through her locker. A pink sweatshirt tumbled to the floor, followed by her car keys.

"Whose name are you talking about?" Alison asked.

"That detective. Remember the eye candy? He and that lady detective came into the restaurant the other day asking about Amber."

"I don't know. I wasn't here," Alison said.

"But Madison Santos was. I have to find her and see if she has that detective's card." Maggie ran past Alison, leaving her locker open with a sweater caught on the door.

Alison picked up the sweatshirt and car keys, then pushed the sweater back into the locker. "What about your tables?" Alison called out as she turned around.

Maggie was already bounding up the stairs toward Madison Santos' office. She knocked rapidly on the door, waiting for Madison's voice to say "come in." When she didn't get a response, her knocking became more frantic. Finally, Maggie opened the door and barged into Madison Santos' office.

Madison looked up from her desk and stopped mid-sentence, as she was speaking to the owners of the Lakota. She quickly covered the mouthpiece with an annoyed look at the intrusion into her office.

"I'm busy, Maggie. Can't this wait?"

The silver car had been parked in the visitors' parking lot of the Lakewood hospital for days when the staff finally noticed it had not been moved in several days. When this information was called into the Lakewood Police Department, security was told it was a rental that had not been returned and that payment had been made using a bogus credit card.

Uniforms were told to secure the car but not to touch the vehicle.

Connor and Kate arrived and pulled on latex gloves before examining the car's exterior. The car was locked, so Connor asked one of the uniforms to use a slim jim. Both detectives stood back and watched the officer pop the lock on the driver's side door. Connor walked over to his unit, opened the trunk, and retrieved the brown paper bag. He again allowed Sundae to sniff Amber Howell's blouse.

Connor pointed toward the silver rental. Sundae ran to the car and jumped inside She sniffed the front seat, then jumped into the backseat. One sniff of the backseat and Sundae began to howl, which meant only one thing. Sundae had positively identified Amber's scent.

"Get our CSI team out here to check for prints. Also, Kate, ask Sandy to call Mr. Williams. We need him to look at this car and make a positive ID."

Kate noticed the green rental car sticker that Mr. Williams had described.

While Kate was talking to Sandy, she asked her to call the rental car office to find out if they had video of the renter.

CHAPTER 7

The video from the security camera was grainy at best as Kate clicked through frame-by-frame, looking for just the right frame that would help them.

All they needed was to put a face to the build of the male who had rented the silver car that had been dumped and in which Sundae had picked up Amber's scent. The back room where the detectives sat was dimly lit. The light overhead flickered due to the bulb's age or the fluorescent fixture's ballast or both, Connor thought as he glanced up. The room had a stench that Kate kept trying to place but just couldn't figure out.

The car had been rented at a small establishment, not one of the big names. *Probably the reason why the perp picked this place*, Kate thought.

The two detectives, with Sundae at Connor's feet, noted the time stamp on the video from the evening when the silver car had been rented. The car of interest had been rented at approximately 6:50 p.m. according to the rental agreement, a copy of which lay on the old, coffee-stained desk where they sat. However, once the time on the video changed to 6:30, they saw nothing more than a blank screen. No longer could they see the lanky, pimple-faced clerk who had been behind the counter. They saw nothing but a black screen. Connor's brow furrowed in frustration.

"Run it back. Maybe we missed something," he said, rubbing his hand over the stubble on his face.

"The same thing happened at the Gold and Silver Shop when one of Amber's credit cards was used." Kate's voice echoed Connor's frustration.

Regardless, Kate ran the video back and again they saw the same blank screen.

Connor grabbed his cell phone. "Sandy, this is Connor. Has our CSI team been able to pick up any soil samples from the underside of the rental car or from the carpets inside the car? DNA? Anything? We've got nothing from the video at Right Ride Rental Car. It goes dark just before the time of the rental, like the video at The Gold and Silver Shop did. Oh, can you ask our technical people to take another look at The Gold and Silver Shop's video? Tell them I'll bring back a copy of this one. One more thing, Sandy. Ask them if they know how this guy is pulling this off ... blocking the video feed. This guy is slick!"

"Connor, the Howells just received an email," Sandy said. "They said it was sent from Amber's email account."

"Amber sent an email?"

"That's what they said. They're on their way over with a copy."

"No … call the Howells back. Tell them we'll have one of our geeks go to the house. Call our tech people and have them inspect the email. Kate and I will head over there as soon as I can get a copy of this video. Oh, and thank you, Sandy."

"Will do," Sandy said.

Connor disconnected the call and turned to Kate. "The Howells got an email from Amber," he said to Kate.

"Do you…?"

Connor interrupted her. "I doubt it was from her. Just a gut feeling."

Kate sat thinking, running her hand through her auburn hair, wondering how the male person of interest had managed to block out the video and leave no trace behind. Criminals always messed up. From her years of experience, she knew that they always made a mistake at some point – leaving something behind, a print, an image caught on some store's video…

"That's it!" Kate quickly stood up from the old wooden chair. Sundae became alarmed and stood, looking at Kate, waiting for a command.

"What's *it*?" Connor asked.

"Let's go!" Kate grabbed the rental agreement and exited the tiny back room. Connor and Sundae followed.

"Did you find any...?" The clerk stopped mid-sentence as he watched the detectives go out the front door.

Kate didn't stop until she was on the sidewalk, looking from left to right.

"Kate, what are you looking for?" Connor asked.

"You take that side of the street; I'll take this side. He may be slick enough to remove the video from where he goes in, but can he do it if other cameras are in the area?"

Connor grabbed his cellphone and called Detectives Bob Barton and Grant Harris. He asked them to revisit the area in and around The Gold and Silver Shop and do the same thing he and Kate were doing. Maybe between the two establishments, just maybe, they could find something, anything to put it all together.

Kate and Connor split up, each taking a different side of the street. First, Connor turned back to ask the clerk if he could make a copy of the video.

"Just take this one." The kid tossed the video to Connor. "We record over them after a week anyway." The clerk watched Connor grab the video and leave with Sundae.

Connor looked around the area. It was a

rundown section of downtown where the business storefronts were not kept up. He saw a hardware store and five rows of storage. On his side of the street were several other businesses, whose windows were boarded up; clearly, the companies were no longer in business.

First, Connor entered the hardware store next to the car rental office. The clerk just chuckled when Connor identified himself and asked if they had security video on the premise.

The storage facility had video but nothing that pointed in the direction of Right Ride Rental. As Connor stepped out of the storage facility, Kate crossed the street, shaking her head.

Heading toward the car, Connor let Sundae climb into the backseat, then got in himself.

"Now what? We have a dead end again," Kate said.

"We're heading to the Howells to check out that email." As Connor started backing out, his cell phone rang.

"Maxwell."

"Detective, this is Maggie."

"Maggie?" Connor asked.

"Yes. Remember, the waitress where Amber worked?"

"Yes, Maggie."

"You told me to call if I remembered anything. Well, I did."

CHAPTER 8

"This is probably nothing," Maggie said nervously. "There was a customer here last week who was quite charming and a big tipper."

Connor pulled back into his original parking space and put the call on speaker so Kate could hear.

"I understand … but charming and big tipper don't really mean much," Connor said.

"Detective, he wouldn't allow anyone else but Amber to wait on him. I tried, but he told me he wanted only Amber. It seemed weird, I guess."

"Do you or your manager know his name?"

"No."

"Have you seen him since Amber went missing?" Connor asked.

"No. Maybe because she's not here, he no longer eats here. I don't really know for sure."

"Did he pay with cash or a card?" Connor asked.

The line was silent for a few seconds.

"I think it was always cash, but because I never waited on him, I can't be sure."

"Can you check with your manager about this? As you stated, he never allowed anyone but Amber to wait on him, so maybe he paid with a card. If we could get his name, we could check on him," Connor said.

"As far as I know, it was always cash, from what Amber told me, but I'll check. Also, he would slip Amber a fifty for a tip," Maggie said.

"A fifty?"

"Yes, and on the last visit, he gave her a hundred-dollar bill. Amber was so excited, she came back to the kitchen and showed it to me."

Connor looked over at Kate and shook his head.

"Maggie, do the waitresses always pick up the card or cash for your guest at the table, or do the customers bring it to the register to pay for their meals?" Connor asked.

"We always bring the ticket to the table, then take it to the register for our guests."

Connor thought about this new information for a few seconds.

"Maggie, we're headed over to Amber's parents' place right now. How late will you, Amber's supervisor, and the manager be there today?"

"I have to stay until five. Alison and Madison both leave at four."

"Listen, Maggie." Connor looked at his wristwatch, checking the time. "We'll try to be there before four to talk to you, Alison, and Madison. Would you ask both of them if they could speak with us when we get there?"

The Lakewood CSI team was already analyzing the email when Connor and Kate walked into the Howells' residence. Mrs. Howell was dabbing at tears from her eyes. Both of the Howells looked like they had aged ten years since their daughter's abduction. Even the neat, well-kept, two-story house wasn't the same. The once-clean, well-dusted, shiny tabletops were now filled with newspapers and fliers bearing Amber's face and description. There was also a hand-operated staple gun and a large roll of tape with which to hang up the fliers. Connor thought about how this was the Howells' new normal, at least as of the last few days—if this new way of life could even be referred to as "normal." Nonetheless, it was the way things were now.

"Was the IP spoofed?" Connor asked.

Connor knew that this was a technique a hacker would employ to use another person's IP address to help cover his or her own tracks online. It was much more difficult, if not impossible, for the police and

FBI to track the origin of the communications that were being sent.

Eric Martinez sat at the Howells' desktop computer. He was a third-generation officer with the Lakewood Police Department. Like his father and grandfather before him, Eric had gone through the police academy and done his time as a uniformed patrol officer. Then he transferred to CIS with the IT department.

"No, this appears to have come from her cell phone," Eric responded.

"Can you see where that cell phone pinged off of?"

"I have the team back at the PD doing that right now." Eric handed a printed copy of the email to both Connor and Kate. The detectives read it silently.

Dear Mom and Dad,

I am okay, no need to worry about me. I took some time off to think. I just need to get away from Lakewood for a while. Please understand that I have a lot on my mind. I'm thinking about going back to school, my job, and Tanner.

I'll be in touch.

Love,

Amber

After reading the email, Connor and Kate sat down with the Howells. Mrs. Howell held her copy of Amber's email as if it was the only thread of hope that her daughter was still alive. The paper rattled as her hands shook.

"Mr. and Mrs. Howell, looking over this email that you received today," Connor looked at the copy in his hand, "can you see any speech patterns or anything at all that would clearly indicate this email was not sent by Amber?"

Mrs. Howell shook her head no, not wanting to believe the email might not have come from her daughter. It was the only hope she had, the only contact from Amber since she'd gone missing.

Kate sat down with Mrs. Howell and put her arm around her as Connor and Mr. Howell stepped into the next room.

"There's one thing I noticed … Amber always signs her texts and emails to her mom and me with 'XOs,' not 'love' at the end of each message. Another thing is that she ends her texts and emails with an A. She never spells out Amber."

Mr. Howell reached into his side jean pocket and pulled out his smartphone. He found the last text message from Amber and showed it to Connor. It was signed just as he had described.

Connor scrolled through several old messages before handing the phone back to Mr. Howell.

"Do you by any chance have an old email that you've saved?" Connor asked.

Mr. Howell quickly looked through his old emails and handed the phone back to Connor. Connor read the email, which talked about a trip to the Howells' cabin. Just like the text messages, it was signed with XOs and closed with an A.

"Detective, she…" Mr. Howell pointed toward his wife, "doesn't want to believe the email isn't from Amber."

"I understand, Mr. Howell. Before we came over here, we received a call that a car had been found. It matches the description of the silver car seen by Amber's neighbor, Mr. Wallace, who said it had been parked by Amber's truck the morning she went missing. I put my K9 into the car and she picked up Amber's scent in the backseat."

"So, you have the guy?" Mr. Howell asked.

"No, the car was dumped. The credit card that the male subject used to pay for it was stolen. Somehow, the card didn't show it was a fraudulent purchase until the car was off the lot," Connor said.

"We've done everything. We've hung fliers, and friends and co-workers have been searching everywhere. My wife and I have stayed in this house, waiting for a ransom call that never comes. My company has put up a large sum of money for information, and nothing! Your department did a polygraph test on both my wife and me, talked to my co-workers, did background checks on us, turned our house upside-down looking for anything. They did the same to her boyfriend, Tanner." Mr. Howell blinked back tears. "For Christ's sake, give us something, anything to hold onto."

"Mr. Howell, in all missing persons cases, we first look into the person or persons closest to the victim to rule out the possibility that they were involved in the victim's disappearance. It's just standard procedure, sir."

"Procedure … what in the hell are you doing to find our daughter? We don't hear anything from you, the department, or the FBI."

"Sir, I can assure you, we're looking into all leads at this time. Everyone has been followed up on."

Connor continued. "Can I ask if you or Mrs. Howell ever heard Amber speak of a man who was a big tipper where she worked before she went missing?

"A big tipper?" Mr. Howell repeated.

"We're looking into someone at Lakota who expressed a lot of interest in Amber at the restaurant.

"No, she never mentioned it to us. Why? Who is this person?"

CHAPTER 9

Connor, Kate, and Sundae got back into their police unit. Leaving the Howells' home, they headed west on Denton and turned onto Kingston, where a steady flow of heavy traffic greeted them: the beginning of rush hour. Connor glanced at his watch. It was exactly 3 p.m. and a sea of taillights was in front of them. He had to get to the Lakota before Alison and Madison left work for the day. Turning right, he came to a stoplight.

Kate glanced out the window at a panhandler on the street corner, holding a cardboard sign. His clothes were tattered and torn while his face showed signs of despair. She rolled down her window. The man limped over to the side of the car as Kate slipped him a five-dollar bill.

"Bless you," said the homeless man.

Sally Wilson had jogged down the ditch bank behind the lumberyard every day for the last three years. She told herself she did this for herself, that this was her time of the day. No calls to answer, no errands to run, no boss to answer to. Just her and the nature that stretched out before her.

Her smartphone pumped the latest tunes through her earbuds. She was in the zone—or, as some runners refer to it, mustering the surge. She ran past the old wooden bridge that spanned the ditch and made a mental note to bring her camera there next time to photograph the old bridge. Her line of vision scanned up ahead to the ditch bank road on which she was running, then back again to the weeds along the embankment.

Just for a second, her peripheral vision caught sight of something. She wasn't sure what, if anything, she'd seen. It was probably nothing, she reasoned with herself. Sally turned around while keeping up her pace, not wanting to alter her heart rate, and ran back to the spot where she saw whatever it was. Running in place, she looked out over the embankment. A chill ran through her and she stopped running, jerking the earbuds from her ears.

An old man working in the lumberyard across the ditch heard the scream over the forklift he was driving. Looking up, he saw a young woman in orange running shorts and a white tank top, screaming on the ditch bank. Quickly, he ran out of the yard across the small wooden bridge and over to the young woman.

"Now, now, it's okay. It's just an old bullsnake," said the man, trying to comfort Sally.

Sally shook her head, but she couldn't speak. The old man assumed she'd encountered one of the large, harmless bullsnakes that roamed the area, which was prime real estate for the snakes.

"No, there!" Sally pointed frantically toward weeds below her on the bank.

"It's probably gone…" The lumber worker said, trying to reassure her that the snake meant no harm.

When his eyes finally made contact with a young woman's brown hair and forehead protruding from the large overgrowth of tumbleweeds, he quickly turned and ran to the body. The woman's skin was chalky and pale, and her eyes were open in a blank stare. Small blood spots had formed in the whites of her eyes. Slightly lifting the tumbleweed, he noticed the woman's unclothed body.

"Oh, Dios Mio!" exclaimed the lumber worker in his native tongue.

Sally knew what that meant: "Oh, my God!" in Spanish. She watched as the man backed away from the body. Sally dialed 911.

Connor's cell phone rang, breaking the silence in the car.

"Maxwell." He put the phone on speaker.

"Detective Maxwell, this is Detective Jamie Kraft with the Natick County Sheriff Department. According to a BOLO issued by your department, you're looking for a young woman by the name of Amber Howell."

"That's correct."

"Detective, I can't be one hundred percent certain, but I believe we may have found her."

"Alive?"

"I'm sorry, no."

Connor quickly turned the police unit around and headed out of the city into the county. "Give me your 20; we'll head right over."

After the detective gave him the location where the body had been found, Connor hooked a U-turn at the next light.

"Call the Lakota and ask to speak to Madison. Ask her if we can meet with them tomorrow," Connor said to Kate. "If not, see if Barton and Harris can go over there.

At 3:50 p.m., Connor pulled off the road. He wished he had a four-wheel drive as they navigated the small, dirt ditch bank road. After parking behind several county sheriff department cars, Connor, Kate and Sundae began walking toward the yellow crime scene tape. TV reporter Candy Martin quickly ran toward them, thrusting out her microphone.

"Can you confirm this is the body of Amber Howell?"

"Candy, I just got here on scene. No comment." Connor walked past the reporter who continued to rattle off questions to deaf ears.

Looking at the parade of news vehicles, with more coming down the ditch bank road, Connor shook his head in disgust.

"The press swarms to a dead body like flies," he said to Kate as he lifted the yellow crime scene tape, allowing Kate, Sundae, and himself to pass under. As the three of them came within five feet of the body, a uniformed sheriff's deputy stopped them. Connor pulled his badge from his belt holder.

"I need to talk to Detective Kraft. I'm Detective Connor Maxwell and this is my partner, Detective Kate Stroup."

Detective Kraft popped his head around the brush below and waved them through. The dead woman's body lay there, dumped like trash. Not even a shallow grave, just tumbleweed to cover her body, Kate thought.

Sundae ran to the body, sat, and howled. Before identifying the body or doing any high-tech testing, Connor gave Sundae the command to search the area. The thirteen-inch tri-colored beagle obeyed.

"We photographed the scene from all angles. From what I can see, detectives, this is your girl.

We're waiting for the ME to get here, but I'd say the Mexican bow tie was the cause of death," said Detective Kraft.

Connor had seen this before. A short strand of barbed wire attached to two wooden dowels was around the woman's neck. Connor knew the Mexican bow tie was one of the most brutal ways a human could die. By the amount of blood that had drained from the barb's puncture wounds, Connor guessed the victim had been kept alive and tormented until the perp gave the final pull, strangling her.

"Did you happen to find any clear shoe prints?" Connor asked.

"There were a few on the other side of the body. We have photos of them that we'll get to your office."

"Would you mind if we called out the CSI team to do a cast?" asked Connor.

"Call them. With the cutbacks in county funding, we don't have the equipment."

CHAPTER 10

Sundae sprinted through the sagebrush, tumbleweeds, and dead wood in a zig-zag pattern, searching the area close to where the body had been found. She looked up only when she heard the ME's van rattling down the old ditch bank road until the brakes screeched to a stop. Quickly, Sundae put her head back down to search. The white tip of her tail was all that could be seen above the dense brush, and much of the time the brush was higher than her raised tail. She came upon a woman's light blue coat and sat beside it. Sundae howled, signaling to Connor that she had found something she believed to be Amber's.

Connor crouched to inspect the garment. He poked at it with a stick.

"Release," Connor commanded as Sundae went back to her task of searching.

"She find something…?" Kate's words trailed off when she saw the coat

Connor looked up at Kate, squinting at the sunshine behind her.

"A lady's coat matching the description of the one Amber was wearing the morning she went missing."

Sundae sat and howled, signaling once again that she had found something. She was about six yards away from the coat. Even standing up, Connor couldn't see what she'd found, as the brush was so thick.

"Can you get an evidence bag and some gloves out of our unit? Bag and tag this; I'll go see what else Sundae found." Connor began walking toward Sundae.

Kate quickly bagged and tagged the coat, noticing bloodstains on it. She walked over to Sundae and Connor.

There, between Sundae's paws, was a black purse. Connor put on the gloves that Kate handed to him and dug through the purse until he found a wallet, which he pulled it out. It was clear to both Connor and Kate that it was Amber's purse and wallet. The ID showed Amber's information and bright, smiling face. The wallet contained no cash or credit cards, just a few photos of friends and family taken in much happier times. They recognized the Howells and Tanner, but there were a few other people whom neither Kate nor Connor knew.

Other items in the purse included half a package of gum, an asthma inhaler, a cell phone case without a phone, tissues, a ticket stub for a movie that had played at the theaters a few weeks ago, and receipts that looked as if they had simply been tossed into the purse after purchases.

Connor held the purse to his nose. "Smells like a medical office or something. I can't place it." He stood and held it up to Kate's nose.

"It does," she agreed.

Sundae ran back to Connor's side, indicating she had found nothing more. Connor finished labeling all the evidence Sundae had discovered and the trio walked back to the body. Malcolm Greenblatt, the Natick medical examiner, was bent over it.

"Anything?" Connor asked.

Malcolm looked up at Connor and Kate. "You know, Maxwell, we really need to stop meeting like this."

"Malcolm, I wish we never had to meet this way. Find anything?"

"As you probably already noticed, the victim has multiple wounds to her forearm. They're clearly defensive wounds. She fought back against her attacker. Some look older than others. My educated guess at this point is that she'd been held against her will for a few days." Malcolm stood and walked toward the victim's head, then crouched down again. "She was strangled, as you can also clearly see. That's indicated by the tiny blood spots in the whites of her eyes. Once I get her back to the office and on the table, I can look into the rest for you."

"Malcolm, I'm sure this is our vic, so I'll have the parents come over and make a positive ID."

"For now, she'll be listed as Jane Doe," Malcolm said.

Beth Ellis, a psychologist and criminal profiler, had once worked with the FBI, but Kate thought she would look more at home modeling on a runway. Beth looked at the meager amount of information the Lakewood Police had gleaned so far. Glancing over her notes, she shook her head, then spoke to the group of detectives, which included Connor, Kate, Bob, and Grant.

"Amber's body was found unclothed but no sexual contact was made, according to the ME's report. This leads me to believe this was meant to be an embarrassment to the family. We typically see this in mob hits. However, you said there's no mob connection to her, the boyfriend, or her family."

"That's correct," Connor stated.

"What about the ex-boyfriend?" Beth asked.

"Grant and I have been trying to find out anything about him. So far, we've failed to locate him or even his name. We have only a description from Maggie, one of Amber's co-workers and also Amber's parents," Bob said.

"The method by which our victim was strangled also leads us to mob connections, mainly the Mexican mafia," Beth said.

"Beth, at this time, we can't see any connection at all to any gang or mob," Kate stated.

Bob Barton paced back and forth in front of the whiteboard, looking for anything.

"What about the current boyfriend, Tanner?" Beth asked.

"He served one tour of duty in Iraq and came home after an honorable discharge from the army," Connor said.

"He doesn't talk about it much," Kate said.

"Usually the ones who did the most, don't," said Bob Barton, a retired Air Force veteran.

Connor stood and passed a written statement he and Kate had gotten from Maggie, the co-worker at the Lakota, to Beth.

"What this states," Connor pointed to the handwritten report, "is that the week before Amber's abduction, a male subject came into the restaurant several times a day to eat or have coffee. He expressed extreme interest in her. Amber's co-worker, who wrote this statement, told us the male refused to let anyone wait on him except Amber, and he was a big tipper. She said he was a charmer, too ... dressed in nice clothes, wore an expensive watch, and tipped her fifty dollars each time, except for his last visit, when he left Amber a hundred-dollar bill," Connor said.

"Do you feel she willingly went with the perp? It would seem the large tips were to win over her trust," said Beth.

"We don't believe so. Traces of the drug ether were found in the rental car. It was also on the purse and around the victim's nose and mouth," Kate said.

"That would certainly aid the perp in abduction and control. At this point, my question is motive. The only motive I can see is money. But why not ask for a large ransom? Surely, the Howells would have paid," Beth said.

"Every step he makes is untraceable. Video at any establishment is blank before he comes in until he leaves. While the money is less than a large ransom, he's after what he can get out of the victim and then he's gone. No fingerprints, no DNA, no video ... we're searching for an enigma." The frustration was apparent in Connor's voice.

The desk phone rang and Kate picked it up. Although only Kate's side of the conversation could be heard, it was clear to Connor that Kate was talking to dispatch.

"Sandy, I'm going to put you on speaker so Connor can hear. Go ahead, Sandy."

"What I was just telling Kate is that I was overhearing the chatter on the county frequency about a missing person. Several hours later, I got a call from the Natick County SO. They believe this was an abduction."

The room became eerily silent.

CHAPTER 11

Connor, Kate, and Sundae drove out to the Natick Sheriff's Department. Detective Jamie Kraft met them in the lobby. Sundae sniffed around, checking out every inch of the room.

"Amazing how she works." Kraft watched the little beagle poke her nose into everything in the lobby.

"Before I requested a K9, I did a lot of research before deciding what breed I wanted. I knew I wanted a scent hound. I didn't want a 90- or 100-pound take-down dog. When I told the department I wanted a Beagle, the chief laughed at me. I asked several times and each time I was told that a beagle wasn't large enough or strong enough to take down a perp. I explained that I wanted detection, a dog with the ability to sniff out things. I finally adopted her on my own and trained her the best I could. Then I started using her. Once the department saw that she was an asset to them, they put her through professional training," Connor explained.

"I was impressed by how quickly she was able to find the things belonging to Amber Howell," Detective Kraft said.

"As far as taking down a perp, she saved my life," Kate said, unconsciously touching her scar from the bullet wound.

"You know, I think I read something about her in the Lakewood newspaper a few months back."

"Yes. She was awarded the PDSA Gold Medal for Bravery," Kate said proudly, looking fondly at Sundae.

"I got her a steak. In all honesty, I think Sundae was more impressed with the steak than the medal," Connor said as he chuckled.

"It sure is amazing how she works," Kraft said.

"I guess I'm still not sure why you wanted to meet with us," Connor said.

"The abduction yesterday is eerily similar to that of Amber Howell. Only this time, the victim's a male. The wife said her husband had recently met some guy. She described him as fancy, a big spender."

"Fancy?" asked Kate.

The detective smiled at Kate. "Detective Stroup, in the county, we're more rural, country folks, very down to earth. The wife was referring to the way the man was dressed, his car, and the way he talked.

She told me from the start that she didn't like the man, nor did she trust him."

"There's no common victimology or sexual component," Connor said, looking over at Kate and Jamie.

"Connor, show him the sketch," Kate said.

Connor reached into his sport coat, pulled out his smartphone, swiped through some photos, and stopped on one. It was a pencil sketch of a man.

"Our perp was known to frequent the Lakota restaurant, where Amber Howell worked. One of her co-workers and her supervisor worked with our department's artist and came up with this sketch."

Connor passed his smartphone to Detective Kraft, who looked over the sketch.

"We can print this out so that you can show it to the wife," Connor offered.

"Detectives, I was wondering if we all could go out to their farm. We can show this to the wife, but could we also have your dog do a little of her magic? Maybe she can pick up the victim's scent. We have a team working around several areas right now, looking for the man. Maybe your four-legged partner could help us. I have a feeling we may be looking for the same perp," Detective Kraft said.

"I think, at this point, it's too early to tell whether this is the same guy," Connor said.

"Well, Maggie did say the guy who expressed interest in Amber was always nicely dressed and drove a BMW," Kate added.

Connor looked over at Kate and then at Sundae. "Let's go to the farm."

Mrs. McCord looked haggard, her eyes bloodshot and teary. She held a tissue in one hand and Connor's smartphone in the other.

Staring at the pencil sketch on the small screen, she said, "Yes, that's him." Julia McCord fought back tears.

"Are you sure?" Detective Kraft asked.

Connor and Kate watched the woman and glanced around the home.

"That's him," Julia said with tears in her eyes.

"Mrs. McCord, do you have a shirt or jacket that your husband wore but that hasn't been washed? We'd like to let Detective Maxwell's dog here have it to see if she can pick up his scent."

"You think he's dead, don't you? Is there something you're not telling me?" Julia's voice cracked as she broke down crying.

"Mrs. McCord." Kate walked over and put her arm around the woman's shoulders to comfort her. "Sundae is a police dog; she may be able to find your husband. Often, in cases like this, they hold a person somewhere. Or maybe your husband got sick in one of the fields. Whatever the case, Sundae is very capable of searching for him. She can do better than a human can," Kate said.

Julia stood and left the room. She returned holding a blue flannel shirt.

"I haven't done laundry. Usually, I would have done it yesterday but when…" Julia sat down, unable to finish her sentence. "I just want him back," she finally sobbed.

Once it had been determined that the man in the sketch was also the man who had recently befriended Julia McCord's husband, the two departments began working together on the two cases.

Julia McCord had told the uniformed deputies who were the first to take the report that she had become suspicious of the man when he had come to the farm. He had told her husband that he had taken a DNA test and had found that they were long-lost cousins. According to her report, Mr. McCord told the man he had never done any DNA testing, but he still took the man's word for it.

The week before he went missing, Garret McCord and the unknown man met everyday for lunch at a café on Highway 10 on the county line. The man had told Garret that his name was Ted McCord and that he really wanted to connect with family members he had discovered from his DNA results.

However, Ted McCord, which was probably an alias, seemed more interested in the McCords' business and money than in being a family member, according to Mrs. McCord. When she expressed concern about the unknown man, Garret told her not to worry. In the report, she stated that the man known as Ted McCord had said he worked for some type of law enforcement, but he hadn't gone into any details.

Both the county and the city of Lakewood ran the name through NCIC and law enforcement databases. Nothing seemed to match. While thousands of men were named Ted McCord, it was a dead end and, more than likely, a false name.

Sundae spent days searching with crews in the fields surrounding the farm and by the café. They found nothing, not even a trace. The TV stations in the area ran the police department sketch during every newscast, along with a tip hotline. Every station had the sketch on its website. Connor knew that if the guy was planning to try anything in the area, he would have to change his looks to avoid detection.

A candlelight vigil was held for both victims. All five of the detectives attended, knowing all too well that the perp usually came to these events and sometimes even helped in the search for the victims. The detectives worked their way around the crowd, studying the sea of faces, looking for anyone who resembled the sketch.

As the evening sunlight gave way to darkness, he walked over to the table on wobbly heels. He lit a candle and then stood and listened. Even covered in nylons, his legs were cold. The ladies' pumps hurt his feet and the dress allowed the chill to flow right up his legs, but this was the only way he could insert himself into the crowd. He had been a member of Amber's search team and had even helped with Garret's until that bitch, Maggie, had given his description to that damn sketch artist who had drawn his nose all wrong.

In the crowd, he spotted Connor. He walked over to the detective's side and stood next to him. Connor glanced at him and then back at the crowd. 'What power,' he thought to himself. 'Here I am, standing not more than a foot away from you, Detective Connor.'

Connor sniffed the air. Something was wrong, but what was it?

CHAPTER 12

Connor walked into the kitchen and removed the head of a large cookie jar shaped like a beagle. A friend had given it to him—or, more likely, Sundae—for Christmas one year. At the sound of the lid being lifted, Sundae darted into the kitchen. Connor reached in and got two small biscuits out of the jar, then placed them in Sundae's food bowl. Connor watched her eat the biscuits and he smiled. In so many ways, he thought to himself, Sundae was just like any other family dog. She had a bed, her blankets, a backyard to run and play in, and her favorite toys: a pink bunny named Pinkie and a small teddy bear named Jack.

Then again, she also had a job she went to each day. With Sundae, Connor did not adhere to the standard of police dogs and their home lives. He knew they both did their jobs well and that was all that mattered.

Connor walked to the back door, switched on the light, and let out Sundae. He sat on the porch, deep in thought; something about the Howell case was bothering him, but no matter what, he couldn't put his finger on it. He tried not to allow his work to encroach on his home life, but with him living alone except for Sundae, it was sometimes hard to separate the two.

What the hell was it? He ran his hand through his thick brown hair. He remembered Beth Ellis, the police psychologist, talking one time about what she termed "mind-pops." She explained them as thoughts or images that unexpectedly pop into the mind and that have nothing to do with the activity the person is engaging in at the time.

"Mind-pops," Connor said to himself. "More like a brain fart."

Connor's mind flashed back to earlier that afternoon, when Detective Kraft's badge had glimmered for a fleeting second without him noticing it.

His eye caught Sundae running toward him, ready to go in and bring him back to the present. Connor stood.

"Come, Sundae, we have an early day tomorrow," he called out as the little beagle ran to him. Reaching down, he petted her. "Time for bed."

Sundae ran inside and toward the back bedroom of the three-bedroom, ranch-style home. By the time Connor had locked the doors and walked into the bedroom, Sundae was already nestled in her bed. Connor covered her with a small pink blanket.

He walked over to the cherry wood dresser and opened the top drawer. There he stood, looking at a framed photo of his wife and himself smiling. He put the photo back and closed the drawer. Connor fell into a fitful sleep as the grandfather clock he had handcrafted several years ago for his wife—now ex-wife—chimed two. Connor tossed and turned in his sleep.

In his restless dreamlike state, Connor's eyes focused on the sheriff's badge of Detective Kraft. Suddenly he was once again a deputy at the Natick Sheriff's Department, just out of the academy and having finished up training with his training officer, Clay Valerio, a seasoned deputy. Connor was in a one-man unit when the call came in from dispatch.

"Officer down, code 3."

Connor had felt the adrenaline race as he drove to the scene. As he exited the car, another deputy rolled to a stop. Next to Clay's car, under an old cottonwood tree, Clay lay curled into the fetal position in a pool of his own blood. Connor drew his Colt 357 Python. The two officers approached the scene with caution. The rookie who had been riding with Clay was on the other side of the car in a sitting position next to the rear tire. His gun was drawn. With his finger on the trigger, he repeatedly pivoted left and right. The rookie's eyes were staring off into the distance. He hadn't been hit but it was clear that he was in a state of shock.

"You okay?" Connor had asked.

The rookie hadn't responded. He'd held his gun in a firing position with his finger on the trigger.

"Put down your gun, Kyle," Connor demanded. "It's okay, we're here."

Kyle lowed his gun.

The other sheriff's officer called out. "Over here!"

Connor took Kyle's weapon from him and ran toward Deputy Jordan.

The perp lay on the ground next to the double-barreled shotgun that had shot Clay.

"He can't breathe," said Officer Jordan.

Connor looked over at Clay, who lay there dead. Then he looked back at the shooter.

"He's been shot. Clay or Kyle must've fired a shot. Went through his forearm and passed through…"

Just then the prep gasped for breath.

"We have to do something. He won't make it until the ambulance gets here. We need to do a tracheotomy."

The two deputies worked on the perp who had killed their fellow officer, using a pocket knife to cut a small opening in his throat. Connor had then grabbed Deputy Jordan's ballpoint pen from his chest pocket. He removed the ink cartridge, poured alcohol on the lower half, and inserted the pen into the man's throat. The perp began to breathe. "Now cuff the bastard," Connor said as he stood and walked away.

Connor tossed and turned until the next part of the night terror took him back to two weeks after Clay had been killed in the line of duty. Connor hadn't been on duty more than fifteen minutes when his car had come under fire.

"123 SO!" he yelled, sitting up, soaked with sweat. Sundae quickly jumped onto the bed and on top of Connor to protect him.

"Sundae, it's okay. Go back to sleep. It was a bad dream." Connor lifted Sundae from the bed and placed her gently back into her own bed. He covered her up then went into the bathroom and splashed cold water on his face. It must have been the deputy's badge that had triggered the nightmare again.

After Connor had been shot, he'd had nightmares for months. But that had been a few years ago. He glanced over at the clock. It was 5 a.m. Too early to get up but too late to go back to sleep. Or was it that he didn't want to relive that nightmare again?

CHAPTER 13

K ate looked on as the elevator door chimed and the door opened. Sundae bounded out and ran to her. Connor slowly stepped out, holding a tray containing two paper cups of hot coffee.

"You look like…"

Kate was interrupted by Connor. "Go ahead and say it," he said as he neared their desks.

He handed Kate her coffee and set his cup on his desk, then tossed the tray into the trash. He hung his sport coat over the back of his chair and slumped his 5' 9" frame into his chair.

"You just…" Kate stopped mid-sentence and looked at Connor's bloodshot eyes. He looked exhausted. "The nightmares again?"

"Don't want to talk about it," Connor said quickly.

Turning his attention to the reports that Kate had put on his desk, Connor saw one that immediately caught his eye. It was marked "Credit Card Thief."

"Mr. Howell's credit card was used for 10K?" Connor lowered the report and looked across his desk at Kate.

"That's what the report says. The uniforms caught the call last night. I already called Mr. Howell. It seems Amber had been carrying his credit card. Apparently, they had forgotten about it when she turned up missing. He said the fraud department called him after the charge was made."

"Where and what was charged?" Connor asked.

"The purchase was for precious metals again."

"Wonderful, another untraceable commodity." Connor shook his head in disgust. "Isn't it enough that the maggot took their daughter's life, dumped her like trash in a ditch?"

"Barton and Harris drove out to Katron County and talked to the metals dealer. The clerk said the man was polite and nothing stood out about him except that he was wearing a lot of cologne or aftershave. The clerk described it to Barton and Harris as he "smelled unusual."

Connor looked up at Kate.

"Smelled unusual...aftershave. That's it! Like he was wearing too much of it," Connor said.

"Connor, what are you talking about?"

"The candlelight vigil last night. A woman was standing right next to me. I thought something was off about her, but I couldn't put my finger on it then. That's it...she smelled like aftershave. Gutsy, he dressed up like a woman and then stood right next to me," Connor explained.

Connor rooted through his files and found Maggie's phone number at the Lakota. He dialed and put it on speaker so Kate could hear.

"Maggie, this is Detectives Connor Maxwell and Kate Stroup. I'm sorry to brother you at work. I know this is going to sound odd, but do you remember whether the guy who frequented the Lakota, Amber's big tipper, wore a lot of aftershave?"

The line went silent for a few seconds. Kate looked on, waiting for Maggie's response. They could hear the clang of dishes and silverware in the background, as well as people talking.

"Yes, as a matter of fact, I do remember. He wore a lot. We used to joke that his aftershave showed up before he did and stayed after he left."

"Maggie, did you recognize the scent, by any chance?" asked Connor.

"Funny you should ask. None of us had ever smelled it before. I even asked Amber once what it was, but she told me she had no idea."

"Maggie, since Amber was killed, has a woman come into the Lakota smelling like that aftershave?" Connor asked.

"Detective, the big tipper was a man, not a woman."

"I realize that. I was just wondering. Think…" Connor said.

The line went silent again.

"I haven't had a woman smelling like that in here. I'll ask around and see if anyone else has. If so, I can call you back."

Connor disconnected the call and sat deep in thought. Then he looked up at Kate.

"Let me guess. The video at the place where the man wearing the aftershave purchased the metals went dark a few minutes before he entered, right?" Connor said.

"You got it."

The four detectives spread out during Amber Howell's funeral. Connor had talked to each of them, explaining that the metals dealer who had sold the gold had said the man smelled heavily of aftershave. He also told them about the woman at the vigil who also smelled of aftershave. His gut feeling was that the man was now dressing like a woman.

Connor thought to himself that this guy was no amateur.

Bob Barton was dressed as one of the funeral directors, in a black suit, white shirt, and black tie. The funeral home had given him a name tag. Bob took up a position in the back of the large chapel.

Connor was behind a front louvered panel where a choir would enter. In essence, it kept him out of sight but gave him the opportunity to survey the sea of faces in the chapel. He looked at his watch as people poured into the chapel. Still nothing.

Harris stood at the entrance of the chapel, also dressed as a funeral director. He greeted the people and then asked them to sign the guest book upon their entrance. Kate placed herself midway through the chapel at the end of a pew so that she could get out quickly if necessary. The Howells had been told that the detectives would be there during the chapel service as well as during the burial at the cemetery.

Connor found his thoughts wandering. Because the perp had been at the candlelight service for Garret McCord the previous night, did that mean he'd already killed Garret and disposed of his body? Or had he left Garret still alive someplace?

Just then, the minister took his place at the front of the chapel behind the lectern. Connor glanced over at Mr. and Mrs. Howell, then at Amber's boyfriend, Tanner. From Connor's perspective, which was not more than 10 feet away, he could see their expressions of pure pain at the loss of their daughter and girlfriend. Amber's coworkers, her supervisor, and the manager of the Lakota sat behind the Howells. Friends and family packed the chapel; however, the male perp with the aftershave, dressed in a male or female's clothes, was not among the crowd—at least not that any of the detectives could see. Had the chameleon once again eluded them, Connor wondered, or had he simply changed into another disguise?

The service lasted forty-five minutes. People passed by the closed casket and shook hands or hugged the Howells as well as Tanner. Connor watched carefully to see if anyone held back in the pews and did not pass by the casket. He saw no one. The pallbearers came forward and carried out the metal casket, which they then respectfully placed into the hearse. Bob Barton took his place behind the wheel of the hearse and Grant Harris rode along. Kate and Connor got into separate cars that weren't their usual units and took their places in the procession. Once at the gravesite, the detectives fanned out. Connor left Sundae in the unmarked car with the window down. The minister gave a short graveside sermon as the Army Honor Guard paraded toward the casket.

Connor noticed a woman behind the crowd; she seemed to be watching the Howells more than the service. Could that be him, dressed as a woman again? Connor tried to remember. If only he could get closer and try to detect the aftershave. Slowly, Connor rotated his position, one person at a time. The woman looked up just as he took his latest position. For a brief second, their eyes met. Connor acted like nothing was wrong. When her glance returned to the Howells, he moved one person closer.

The Army Guard began folding the American flag that was to drape over Amber's casket. Connor moved closer as the flag was presented to Amber's father. Amber's mother broke down as Tanner held her.

The woman looked up as Connor took a step closer. The Honor Guard took its first of three volleys of shots. The woman turned to leave, and Connor followed. Looking back, the woman saw Connor. She stopped, bent down, and took off her heels. She began running, with Connor in pursuit.

He called out to Sundae, "Give chase!"

The perp had at least a one-hundred-yard lead on Connor. Sundae dove out of the car window and hit the ground at a dead run, then quickly closed the gap between herself and the woman.

The wig flew off the man's head. Sundae stopped and shook the hairpiece between her teeth.

"Give chase!" Connor commanded.

Kate saw Sundae and Connor running across the cemetery lawn, dodging headstones. Bob and Grant saw the same thing and joined the chase. Due to the second and third volleys of shots, the crowd didn't seem to notice the detectives sprinting after the wigless woman, nor did they hear the beagle baying as she ran after the man.

Sundae caught up to him and sank her teeth into his one of his ankles.

"Get away from me, you mutt!" the man screamed as he almost fell.

He kicked the beagle, sending her rolling backward onto the grass. Once Sundae was no longer attached to his leg, he ran out of the cemetery and onto Main Street

"Get out of my way," he yelled, weaving through pedestrians and pushing them out of his way.

Connor and Sundae entered Main Street and Connor quickly put his badge case on his suit jacket pocket. People stopped, stunned to see a barefoot man in a dress running past them. Connor's head bobbed left and right to see around people as he and Sundae pursued their mark. When the male got to the intersection of Main and Second Streets, he stopped. He dug into the purse he was carrying, pulled out a gun, took aim, and fired one shot at Connor.

"Gun!" Connor yelled out. "Get down!" People scrambled to find cover, as did Connor.

Screams echoed down the street just as Kate, Bob, and Grant descended the hillside from the cemetery onto Main Street. The wigless man, followed closely by Sundae, darted quickly between the heavy traffic and out of sight.

CHAPTER 14

The sounds of a gunshot and the screams it elicited in response carried through the streets. The wigless man ran into traffic as horns honked. People rolled down their windows and yelled at him until they saw he was carrying a gun. Sundae ran behind the man, dodging the cars in the rush hour traffic on Second Street. A man was driving a large, dusty, red two-ton truck, hauling a trailer behind it. He slammed on his brakes and skidded to a stop, nearly hitting Sundae when she managed to grab ahold of the wigless perp's leg and sink her teeth into it.

"Let go of me, you traveling flea circus!" he yelled at Sundae while kicking his leg, trying to free himself from the teeth locked around his ankle. Sundae refused to let go. The perp leveled the gun and took aim at her.

Kate, Bob, and Grant unholstered their weapons. Each of them took cover in a shop's doorway, then traveled forward one doorway at a time. "Visually scan, wait, and move." That was the protocol for each detective. As Kate cleared one doorway, the next detective moved to where she had been standing. Then the next followed.

Shopping bags, food, and spilled drinks started covering the sidewalk as people scrambled for cover. Their faces showed terror as the detectives inched their way past them. A homeless woman hid behind her overturned shopping cart. Its contents – everything she owned – lay across the sidewalk. The homeless woman saw Kate and her badge, gave her a toothless smile, and pointed Kate in the direction from which the shot had come. Silently, Kate motioned with her hand for the woman to stay down.

The second they heard the shot, shop owners locked their doors and turned off their lights, then hid behind desks or displays, or in back rooms. Some store owners helped customers out through back doors. Kate thought about how this was the new standard by which everyone lived today. Sadly, there were too many scenes like this across America.

Kate heard sirens in the distance. She had radioed in and assumed that Connor may have, too, if he'd had the chance. She looked around the doorway of Lakewood Jewelers, then moved one store closer.

A man was slumped next to a lamppost. Kate blinked; the adrenaline was pumping through her veins and her heart was beating so loudly, it pulsed through her ears, which she felt would burst. Was that Connor? She recognized the dark black suit he had worn for the funeral that day. Had the bullet hit him? Where was Sundae? She should have been at Connor's side. The dark brown hair matched Connor's, but the man wasn't moving. His back was turned toward Kate and against the pole.

Then Kate saw a dark boot sticking out from the leg of the black suit. It had to be him. Connor always wore his Western boots. He had trouble finding shoes that fit his feet, with their 4E width. When he was still a uniformed officer, and well before he and Sundae had teamed up, the guys at the PD had nicknamed him Duck Foot. Once Connor had made detective and teamed up with Sundae, the department started called him Charlie Brown, as he was always with his beagle.

Kate's mind was in overdrive. She took a deep breath as she scanned the area. The wigless male was nowhere in sight. Bob came up to her in the doorway.

"Isn't that Connor?" he asked in a whisper.

Kate nodded. "I think so. Stay here and cover me."

Kate ran to the pole. It was Connor.

"You okay?" Kate leaned in and helped him up.

He stood, brushing off his black suit and shaking his head in frustration. "I lost him, dammit, I lost him. I was so…close."

Kate motioned for the other detectives to come. She looked around the streets as their backup screeched to a halt. The media came next.

"Sundae…where's Sundae?" Connor asked, anxiously looking around. Exhausted, he spun in all directions, starting with the direction where he had last seen the wigless man and Sundae running. Then Connor stopped. "He darted out into traffic. Sundae must've followed him. Get one of the units to go north on Second Street. I'll head south and call her," he said to Kate. "Bob and Grant, one of you head back to the cemetery and pick up that wig and the heels. Maybe we can get something off them to ID this jerk!"

Kate lifted her wrist and talked into her mic. "49 PD, send out a BOLO. K9 Officer Sundae is missing at this time. Also, the unknown male we were chasing was not apprehended. Last seen wearing a black woman's dress, no female wig. He was last seen heading north on Second Street. PD, he is armed and should be approached with extreme caution. He is about five-foot-ten or eleven, medium build with brown hair."

"10-4. 49, is everyone okay?"

"10-4. We will be once we find our missing K9 officer."

Connor quickly turned and crossed the street, calling out to Sundae. "Sundae, come! "Sundae, come!" Kate did the same.

As Connor passed the oncoming cars, he yelled out, asking if they'd seen a beagle. Each passerby shook their head no.

CHAPTER 15

The news van with the station's large, colorful call letters was the backdrop as Candy Martin, news reporter for Channel 7, held her news mic in her hand while a woman touched up her makeup and fussed over her hair. The woman was prepping Candy for her breaking news segment. Gradually, onlookers began coming out of the shops. The "open" signs lit up again and doors unlocked for business. A crowd began gathering by the news van, its members tilting their heads around the people in front of them so that they could get a better look at the newswoman. Candy read from some notes, then handed them back to her assistant.

"One, two, three," a man said as Candy stood before the newsroom camera.

"This is Candy Martin, live on the corner of Second and Main. We have just learned that the Lakewood Police gave foot chase to a suspect from the Lakewood Cemetery this afternoon. The chase ended in gunfire here at the corner of Main and Second Streets."

The news camera panned around the Second Street business area.

"It all started when police noticed a suspicious person attending Amber Howell's funeral. You'll remember that Amber Howell was the victim abducted from her apartment several weeks ago.

"Several detectives from the Lakewood Police Department, along with one K9 officer, were involved in the chase. The subject ran from the cemetery to Main Street. At the corner of Main and Second, he brandished a weapon and shot at one of the detectives. The subject was last seen running into traffic on Second Street during rush hour. The Lakewood K9 pursued the subject and neither has been seen since the incident. The subject was dressed as a woman in a black dress. Detectives believe he dressed this way to disguise himself. Lakewood Police detectives have also told us the subject will have several bite marks on his ankle from his first encounter with the K9 in the cemetery. The subject is approximately six feet tall, with short, dark brown hair and dark brown eyes."

The TV camera cut away to a composite drawing of the subject, created earlier that week by the Lakewood Police sketch artist.

The station returned to Candy Martin. "Police tell me this man is considered armed and extremely dangerous. If you have seen him, please call the tip line at the bottom of the screen. This man may dress as a woman to disguise his looks."

Candy then faded to a photo of Sundae. "The Lakewood K9, Sundae, has been missing since this incident took place. Police have canvassed the area in and around where the shooting took place and where the subject was last seen. They haven't found the subject or the Lakewood K9, Sundae. If you have any information about the whereabouts of this subject or the Lakewood Police Department's K9, again, please contact the hotline across the bottom of your screen.

"Next, we have a young man who was on Main Street when all of this took place." Candy shoved her mic in front of a young man's face for an interview.

Connor was walking down an alleyway between Third and Margett. He saw a drunk sitting next to a dumpster. His clothes were dirty and torn.

"Have you seen this guy or a little tri-colored beagle come through here this afternoon?" Connor held out his smartphone, which contained a photo of the sketch. The drunk studied the photo carefully for about 20 seconds, then made a clicking sound with his mouth.

"No, but as a matter of fact, I saw Superman fly through here about fifteen minutes ago," he said. "Really, he buzzed right past me. You know, I think he has a thing for Wonder Woman." The drunk took another sip from his bottle.

"Really, Superman? Guess Lois Lane better not find out about Wonder Woman," Connor said as he walked away.

"Lois who?" asked the drunk.

Kate had returned to Second Street when a uniformed officer pulled up to the curb. "Detective Stroup," he called out through his opened window. "A lady gave me this." He held up Sundae's collar. One side of it had a leather pouch that held Sundae's ID, while the other side contained her badge.

Kate took Sundae's collar. "Did she see Sundae?" Kate asked.

The uniformed officer shook his head. "I took a report, got her name and everything. I'll have the desk sergeant put it on your desk when I get back to the PD so you and Connor can follow up. Detective, I'm sorry about Sundae."

Kate held onto Sundae's collar, her mind racing in a million directions. What if the perp had Sundae? What if he did something to her? The man clearly had no regard for human life; what would he do to a dog he didn't even know? A dog that had bitten him…

Connor would never forgive himself. Kate had to radio him and let him know that Sundae's collar had been found.

The Lakewood Police Department helicopter

had taken to the sky shortly after the reports that shots had been fired and the release of the perp's description. Four hours later, there were still no sightings of the perp or Sundae. Bob and Grant had retraced the cemetery lawn. They'd found the heels that the perp had tossed as well as the wig. They bagged and tagged each item, which they would later turn over to the lab to see if the heels and wig revealed any information about who the man was. Bob walked the lawn back to Main Street, hoping that something else had been dropped during the chase. He thought for a minute. 'What we need is Sundae doing her zig-zag search that only she's able to do.' Sundae was always so eager to help the department. Now she needed them to help find her. One thing was certain: If they could find Sundae, she would know the perp's scent and that would be a benefit. If…

Bob reminded himself that *if* was sometimes the biggest word he knew.

CHAPTER 16

The old TV set sat atop a thrift-store-find bookshelf in a darkened living room. Carlos Sanchez, age seven, was on the floor watching cartoons. He lay on his belly with his legs folded at the knees. He swayed back and forth to the background music, his right wrapped protectively around the dog lying beside him. Carlos had lived with his grandmother since he was three years old. His nana had taken him in after his mother had been arrested for drug procession and prostitution. As for his father, Jose Diego, Carlos had rarely seen him since Carlos' mother had gone to jail.

Carlos loved living with his nana. There was always a soft bed and a hot meal on the table. Plus, her house was warm in the winter and cool in the summer. Never once did dishes crash against the wall or did he hear screaming and yelling. His nana spoke little English; however, Carlos was fluent in both English and Spanish.

The cartoons ended and the early edition of the evening news came on. The news anchor started talking about the shooting that had taken place at Main and Second Streets two days earlier. An artist's sketch of the man they were looking for appeared on the screen. The anchor segued to the missing Lakewood Police Department's K9, Sundae. Carlos looked at the TV screen, then turned and picked up his dog's head. Biscuit looked at him through sleepy eyes.

Sundae, the tiny beagle, perked up immediately and looked at Carlos. "Is your name Sundae?" Carlos asked.

The beagle tilted her head from side to side.

"Mi hijo." Nana entered the living room. Carlos quickly turned off the TV so his grandmother would not see the beagle on the screen. "You need to do your homework. Did you put up some more posters today about the doggie you found?"

"Yes, Nana," Carlos replied.

What he didn't say was that the posters he'd made last night were currently in the dumpster of a drug store he'd passed on his way home from school.

Carlos had always wanted a dog. From the age of three, he'd been asking Santa for one. His prayers had been answered two days earlier, when Carlos found Biscuit lying in an alley. At first, he thought she was dead but the more Carlos talked to her and petted her soft coat, the more she came around. When Carlos told his grandmother how he had found her, she thought maybe a car had hit the dog.

The beagle had no tags or collar, so Carlos carefully carried her home. Nana gave him a few dollars so that he could go to the corner drug store and get some dog food. Standing in the pet aisle, Carlos looked at the dog beds, collars, and toys. He wanted to buy his new dog a toy. Looking at the money in his hand, he knew he had enough for only the bag of dog food.

An employee saw him standing there. "Can I help you find anything?"

Carlos shook his head. He explained to the lady that he'd just gotten a dog and that he'd wanted one for so long. The lady asked Carlos to wait. She went into a back room and returned a few minutes later carrying a dog bed, a collar, a leash, and a few toys. Carlos watched as she put them on the counter.

"I can't afford to buy anything but the dog food," Carlos said.

"Our dog passed away about a month ago. I couldn't bring myself to get rid of her things. I know Biscuit would want your doggie to have her things."

"Thank you," Carlos said as he filled his arms with all the things for his new dog.

On the walk back to Nana's house, Carlos decided to name his dog Biscuit, just like the lady's dog. When he got home, he excitedly explained to Nana what the lady at the store had told him and how she had given her dog's things to his doggie.

On the second day, Biscuit was feeling much better. She still had a lump on the side of her head but she was much more active. When Carlos got home from school, she ran to greet him with her tail wagging. However, when she heard a police siren, she ran to the front door and scratched at it. Sundae associated the sound with Connor and the department. She knew she belonged back with them.

Carlos didn't realize that Biscuit was probably the missing police dog until after he saw the TV news. He knew he should take her back. After all, he hadn't done anything wrong; he'd only helped the little beagle. Nevertheless, he had waited so long for a dog. How could he give her up?

Nana had told him that if no one claimed her in a week, he could keep her but it was his responsibility to take good care of her. That night, Carlos picked up Biscuit and put her in his bed. As he pulled the covers over them, he told Biscuit how much he loved her and that in five days, he could keep her forever. However, he couldn't let Nana find out who Biscuit really was. With that thought, he petted Biscuit's head and stroked her long, soft ears until she was fast asleep.

Just after 2 p.m., Nana heard a knock at the

door. She opened it part way. Jose forced the door the rest of the way open.

"Where's the kid?" he demanded.

Nana tried to close the door but Jose overpowered her and entered the house. He looked around. Sundae, who had heard the yelling, bounded into the living room.

"He's not here, Jose. He's in school. Now leave," she yelled at him.

Nana looked over at the phone on her old, stained end table.

"The kid's mine. I can do whatever I want with him!" Jose yelled.

"I thought you were still in prison."

"Stop with the questions, old lady," Jose said.

Sundae watched the exchange between the two.

Nana looked at the clock on the wall. "He won't be back until after three."

"You got anything to eat, old lady?"

Nana walked into the kitchen and opened the refrigerator. With the door blocking Jose's view, she took the phone and pressed 911. Nana quickly gave her address, then laid the receiver on a small table so the 911 operator could hear everything.

"Hurry," Jose called from the living room. "I'm hungry!"

He walked through the kitchen door and saw Nana preparing a sandwich. Then he saw that the phone was off the hook. Jose became outraged and grabbed the woman around the throat in a chokehold. Sundae launched herself at Jose, her teeth tearing into his arm. He loosened his grip on Nana and then ran out of the house when he heard the sound of approaching sirens.

The police arrived and Nana told the uniformed officer what had happened. He informed her that Jose had managed to exchange bracelets with another inmate who was due to be released; that was how he'd gotten out of jail.

"The doggie saved me." Nana pointed toward Sundae.

The uniformed officer took down the report as Nana rubbed her neck. Another officer entered the house and informed them that Jose had been found hiding in a backyard two houses down.

It was a slow news day when Candy heard the report of an escaped inmate being captured. She decided to take the news crew over to the house. Candy persuaded an officer outside the door to allow her to ask the woman if she would grant an interview. Then she saw Sundae. Candy looked at the beagle several times before pulling out her cell phone, She swiped until she found the photo of Sundae on their website. Sure enough, the dog in front of Candy was Sundae.

"Officer, may I speak to you for a second outside?" Candy asked.

"Would you excuse me?" the officer asked Nana.

He and Candy left the living room and stepped outside.

"How in the hell did you get inside?" asked the officer.

"Officer, that dog inside is the missing K9 for Lakewood PD."

"What…?"

The officer didn't say another word. He went back inside.

"Your dog." The officer looked at the beagle again. "How long have you had her?"

"Only three days. My grandson found her and brought her home."

Sundae looked out the open front door. Seeing two police cars, she bolted out the door and ran to the first uniformed police officer, then to the next. When she didn't see Connor or Kate, she began running down the sidewalk. Carlos had just come around the corner. In just a few seconds, he saw the police cars by Nana's house, the open door, and Sundae running.

"Biscuit, come back!" he cried out. "Biscuit, come back!" Then Carlos remembered that her real name was Sundae. However, it was too late. Sundae had rounded the corner and was out of sight.

"Sundae, come back!" Carlos cried out.

CHAPTER 17

The house was empty without her. Sundae's bed still sat in the corner along with her small pink blanket, her teddy bear (named Jack), and her pink stuffed bunny, appropriately named Pinkie. Connor wondered if Sundae was alive and if she missed him.

When Sundae and Connor had gone through their K9 training, their training officer had been adamant that the handler—in this case, Connor—should not treat the K9, Sundae, as a pet. The trainer used the example of an officer who was married. The wife may put restrictions on the K9, such as "don't get on the bed" or "don't jump on the furniture." Those commands might be confusing, as the dog would perhaps have to jump on things while on the job. He further stated that the dog should be able to follow its nose. The trainer felt strongly that an off-duty K9 should be kept in a kennel, which the department would issue. A bored off-duty K9 made for a harder working K9 on duty.

Ignoring that advice, Connor had adopted Sundae and brought her into the house. She was given a bed, blankets, and toys. He started her training on his own, from books and what he learned from other handlers. Connor had never experienced a problem with Sundae due to their living arrangements. The fact was, Sundae was part of his own family as well as the Lakewood Police Department family.

Connor was now playing Monday morning quarterback. He wondered if, by treating Sundae like a pet, he'd made her more vulnerable to being picked up by a stranger and brought into a home, disappearing without a trace. Connor walked over to her bed. The night she'd gone missing, he'd been given her collar and police ID. He had laid it in the bed, assuring himself that she would return home. He knew that if she could get loose from the perp or the well-meaning dog lover, she would find her way home. But if she was...

He could never get past that part of his internal dialog. The fact was, he couldn't even bring himself to think about that scenario. Nevertheless, in the back of his mind, he knew he wanted her home no matter what. He had to have closure.

There was an awkwardness at work when he walked through the halls. Co-workers danced around the fact that Sundae was missing.

Connor reasoned with himself that they didn't want to bring attention to her disappearance, as if that would make the pain of losing her easier on all of them. Just yesterday, a uniform had come in talking about the man in the Amber Howell case. The officer had started saying Sundae's name, then stopped himself midway. The look on his face was that of a man who, if he could take back the last few seconds would have done so.

Mr. and Mrs. Howell had called Kate to express how awful they felt. They had come to like Sundae and they simply had no words to express how sorry they were. Both Kate and Connor took posters with Sundae's photo on them to veterinarians, dog parks, and pet food stores. The news media displayed Sundae's photo on their websites and during newscasts. However, as the days passed, they had cut back on the showings. Tips came in and were followed up in both the Howell and McCord cases. The main focus of the case was the perp. To date, McCord's whereabouts—or body—had yet to be discovered.

Something was bothering Sherrie Andrews. It was one of those things that didn't make sense. Sitting at her desk, she flipped through the notes she had written on a yellow legal tablet, trying to figure out what it could be. The notes were references for herself. Sherrie had worked at the bank for only two days. It was a gnawing feeling, like she'd forgotten to lock the door, turn off the burner on the stove, or shut the garage door before leaving for work. But why did nothing come to mind? She opened her drawer and tucked the tablet back into her desk.

Another teller with several people in her line asked Sherrie to help a customer access her safety deposit box. Sherrie retrieved the key for the gate that prevented people from wandering back into the area. Before she opened the gate to the safety deposit box area, she requested an ID. Sherrie carefully examined the ID, then thumbed through the list of names and box numbers. After collecting the customer's key and the bank's master key, she headed toward the box.

"Would you like to use one of our locked rooms?" Sherrie asked in a professional manner.

It was then that she remembered seeing a man on TV the other night—the man who was a person of interest. For what, she couldn't remember. Having started a new job, she was barely able to keep up with the TV shows she followed, let alone the news.

"That's it!" she exclaimed, her words startling the customer she was helping.

"What's it?" asked the customer with a confused look.

"I'm sorry. Just something I had in the back of my mind and I figured it out…I think."

The customer quickly opened her deposit box and dropped an envelope into it, still wondering about the ditzy person helping her. Sherrie quickly put away the list, then followed the customer out and locked the gate behind her. She knew she had to find her manager and tell her that she thought the person whom Candy Martin had shown on TV had been in the bank yesterday.

Several minutes later, Sherrie and the manager sat looking over the list of safety deposit box owners.

"This is my handwriting." Sherrie leaned forward in her chair to point at the entry she'd made on her first day of work. Her hand shook, as she feared she had done something wrong and was going to lose her job. She reasoned with herself; how could she have known that the Lakewood Police Department was looking for this man, a box holder at the bank? *If* this was even the man they were seeking.

"You said that last night you saw on the news that the police want this man or wish to talk to him?" The manager felt her blood pressure rising as she looked at the name on the master list of box holders.

"Yes," Sherrie said.

The manager began tapping on her keyboard, trying to locate the news channel's website. She found a segment with Candy Martin, showing the photo of the Lakewood Police Department K9 that was missing. That couldn't be it. Then she found the

Lakewood Police Department sketch. Turning her monitor around to Sherrie, she asked, "Is this the man who was in here?"

Sherrie shook her head as she glanced at the words "shots fired." The manager looked at the entry that Sherrie had pointed to.

"We put a fraud alert on the McCords' checking and savings accounts, but I guess the family forgot about the safety deposit box. He had a key and the name on the ID matched?" asked the manager.

"He had the key and the name did match or I wouldn't have let him in."

"Did he put something in or take something out?"

"I…I really don't know. I asked if he needed a room to go through his things. He said yes. I tried to lift the box, but it was really heavy. He asked if he could help, so I let him lift out the box. It did feel lighter when he brought it back. He had put some things into one of those cloth shopping bags. I didn't notice it until…" Sherrie's eyes filled with tears. "Is this my fault?"

The manager quickly dialed the Lakewood Police Department and asked to speak to the detectives in charge of the McCord missing person case.

CHAPTER 18

Candy Martin was busy working on her evening report. The news was in her blood and wherever there was a story, she chased it. Candy was about to leave her desk when a call came into her desk phone.

"Martin." Candy listened but heard nothing. She was about to hang up when a timid female voice came on the line.

"Ms. Martin, I watch your show all the time. You said they're still looking for Amber Howell's killer and they haven't found Garret McCord's body."

"Yes, that's correct. Do you have information about the cases?" Candy grabbed a ballpoint pen and writing pad, eager to jot down any news this woman could provide.

The line went silent for a few seconds.

"Are you still on the line?" Candy asked,

brushing her free hand nervously through her naturally blonde hair.

"Yes…I'm sorry. I'm just scared, but I think I may know who it is," said the woman, her voice shaking.

"Have you called the Lakewood Police Department?" Candy asked.

"No, ah…I dated him for a while but he was weird…sorta freaky. He would disappear and then show up weeks later."

"Sounds weird, I agree, but that doesn't mean he's the man the police are looking for," Candy said. "You know the Lakewood Police Department has a hotline, don't you?"

"Ms. Martin, I found ropes, duct tape, a stun gun, and barbed wire in his SUV," said the woman quickly.

"Can you give me your name and phone number so we can follow up?" Candy's hand hovered over the writing pad.

"My name, no. I'm afraid he'll come after me. His name is Dustin…Dustin Rodney. He lives at 4465 Hickory Road."

"How do you spell 'Rodney?'" Candy asked, attempting to keep the woman talking and giving more information.

There was a deafening silence as the caller disconnected the call. Candy was left facing a deadline. Tapping her pen on the pad over the name "Dustin Rodney," she thought for a minute.

The reporter wondered if Connor would give her an exclusive on the story. But what if the woman was just another kook calling in? Candy knew she had to contact the Lakewood Police Department regardless. She picked up her cell phone and swiped through her contacts until she came across the phone number.

Then a thought crossed her mind. Instead of dialing the number, she tapped the space bar on her computer. The screen came to life. Candy quickly opened an app on her taskbar and typed in Dustin Rodney's name and known address. Her screen turned a whitish color as the user interface to the app began its search. A blue progress bar flashed across the screen. Next, the screen changed again and asked her to be patient as her background checker dug deep into the life of Dustin Rodney. After a few minutes, three avatars showed up on the screen.

Candy glanced at the three possible matches. Only one resided in Lakewood at 4465 Hickory Road. She clicked on the one at that address. Candy waited another few minutes for any information about Dustin. Finally, her screen regenerated with whatever information the Internet could gather about Dustin. Candy looked over what had been found. There were several social media accounts, one with no security, which meant the public could see anything the man posted. Candy browsed the photos of Dustin and a young woman. She wondered if this was the timid woman who had called her, or if the woman on social media was the caller's replacement.

She began looking through Dustin's posts as well as any comments his friends had left. She wondered why some people left their social media accounts wide open to the public. However, she was glad that Dustin had done so. He had even listed his date of birth, which she already knew by working her magic with her background checker software. His posts had a dark side to them, as he talked about people he didn't like. Dustin had mentioned a past boss and how he hated the man.

He ranted about politics, gun control, and how much he hated the police. One post included a photo of himself sticking out a pierced tongue with a silver ball attached to it. Scrolling through the other posts, Candy found a photo of him showing off his latest tattoo on his chest. The photo depicted a shirtless Dustin with large block letters spelling out the word "evil." On his muscular left shoulder was a tattoo of a gun with the words "The best way to take care of business." On his other shoulder was a tattoo of a hundred-dollar bill.

Candy split her monitor display into two. On the left side was an enlarged photo of Dustin; on the right side was the police artist's sketch of the man wanted by the Lakewood Police. Candy leaned forward, comparing the two. The noses looked similar and the hair color was correct. The eyes seemed off but this was an artist's rendering. With that, Candy closed her browser and put a call into the Lakewood Police Department.

When the call from the branch manager of the Lakewood Bank and Trust came into the Lakewood Police Department, Sandy Curtis was on duty at the dispatch desk. She put the call right through to Connor and Kate. Sandy hoped this was the break they so desperately needed.

Kate took the call, as Connor was driving. They were following up on a tip they'd just received. Kate quickly copied down the information. Looking at her watch, she told the caller they would be there in about ten minutes.

"Please don't let anyone touch the box. We'll need to see any video you may have," Kate said before disconnecting the call. "Turn around," she continued, to Connor. "We need to head over to the Lakewood Bank and Trust."

Connor looked over at Kate, then pulled the unmarked car over to the shoulder of the road and made a U-turn. Several minutes later, the two stood in the lobby of the Lakewood Bank and Trust. Brooke Walter, dressed in a form-fitting business suit, strolled out to meet them.

"Hi, I'm Detective Connor Maxwell and this is my partner, Detective Kate Stroup."

The three cordially shook hands.

"We were told that one of your tellers may have waited on the person we're looking for," Kate said.

"Let's go into my office."

As they stepped into the room, Sherrie Andrews stood. Once formal greetings had been exchanged, Connor and Kate showed the police sketch to Sherrie.

"That's the man. I'm sure of it. However, the name on the ID he showed me was Garrett McCord." Sherrie handed the sketch back to Connor.

Kate pulled out a photo of Garrett McCord that his wife, Julie, had given to them.

"Do you recognize this man?" Kate asked.

"No." Sherrie studied the photo, then shook her head. "I've never seen this person before."

"We would like to have our CSI people come over and lift prints off the safety deposit box. We can have Mrs. McCord bring over her key," Connor said. To himself, he thought, 'Finally we'll have a set of prints.'

"That's the thing. After my manager told me that you didn't want anyone to touch the box, I explained to her that the day this person came in," Sherrie said, pointing at the sketch, "he was wearing a pair of those white gloves."

"White gloves?" Connor asked

"You know, the ones they sell in the drugstores. When he noticed me looking at his hands, he said he was having a flare up of eczema on his hands. My mother has that from time to time, so I didn't think anything about it. I don't think there will be any prints," Sherrie said.

Connor felt his hope being crushed. 'This guy never slips up,' he thought.

"Did you notice whether he took anything out of the safety deposit box?" Kate asked.

"He asked to go into one of our private rooms. When he came out, he had a cloth shopping bag with him and it looked pretty full."

"And the video…did you have time to review it?" Kate asked the manager.

"You're not going to believe this. We did but the video was blanked out during the time he was here, according to the time stamp on our records," Brooke said.

"Yes, we can believe it. He has a device that breaks the transmission from the video feed to the recorder during the time he enters until after he leaves," Kate said.

The branch manager shook her head in disbelief.

Connor's phone rang and he excused himself from the manager's office to take the call. Sandy Curtis explained that Candy Martin had called in a tip that she had received. "It was from a lady who thinks she may have dated the man you're looking for," Sandy said.

After they exchanged business cards, Kate left

the manager's office. "Not to worry; we'll call Mrs. McCord," she said as they all shook hands again.

"Let's go. Candy Martin at the news station just received a tip from a woman who may have dated the guy," Connor said.

CHAPTER 19

Candy Martin ushered Connor and Kate into a private office. There, her laptop computer was open to Dustin Rodney's social media page and the limited information she was able to get from her background app.

"Any more information on your beagle? We've started running her photo again every evening on the news," Candy said.

"No, not yet," Connor said. Sundae's disappearance hurt like an open wound. He didn't need Candy to remind him about it.

She turned around her laptop and showed the two detectives the information she'd been able to dig up on Dustin.

"Were you able to get the woman's name and address?" asked Kate.

"No. Believe me, I tried. She just blurted out Dustin's name and address and that was it.

However, she did mention finding a stun gun, duct tape, rope, and barbed wire in his SUV. She also said he was weird," Candy stated.

Connor thought to himself that the police hadn't mentioned the barbed wire to the news media. The department always withheld some information from the public for situations such as this.

"What do you think? Could this be our guy?" Kate asked, turning to Connor.

Candy leaned over between the two detectives. "I compared these photos."

Kate looked over at Candy's low-cut blouse and thought to herself that if the woman leaned over any farther, there would surely be spillage. She knew that Candy had tried, on numerous occasions, to ask Connor out for a drink, coffee, or dinner. Connor had always declined but now Kate caught him glancing over at Candy, then nervously brushing back his brown hair before refocusing on the computer screen.

Kate felt a smoldering inside herself when she remembered that night last year when she and Connor had kissed. They both knew that if they took their relationship beyond being partners on the job, one of them would have to transfer to another department. It was the Lakewood Police Department's policy. Nevertheless, Kate felt that little green monster called jealousy rear its head within her.

Candy moved the mouse to open another photo of Dustin. Then she opened the Lakewood Police Department's website to the sketch of the perp.

"I can see the resemblance between his photo and the sketch on your department's website. Can't you?" asked Candy, taking her seat again across from the detectives.

Connor and Kate looked closely at both images. Kate began jotting down all the information she could get about Dustin Rodney.

"The caller mentioned Dustin would disappear for days on end, then show back up with no explanation," Candy said.

Kate handed Connor the information she had written down. Connor stepped into the hallway and called the information into dispatch. He asked them to run anything they had on Dustin Rodney and to get back to him ASAP. He then returned to the office, where Candy was showing Kate all the photos of Dustin's tattoos that she had found online.

"He's certainly muscular enough to overpower his victims," Candy said as she and Kate looked at the massive, muscular chest with the word "evil" written in block letters across it. "Here he's holding a gun." Candy pointed to another image.

"Candy, I'd like to ask you to sit on all this information until we can check it out," Connor said. "At this point, the lead may be nothing more than a disgruntled girlfriend or a very active imagination on the girl's part. We need to check things out."

"If I sit on this information, Connor, can I have the exclusive rights to go live once you have something?" Candy asked.

"I need to run this by our chief. We always try our best to not show preference to one news organization over another."

Connor picked up his sport coat and put it on, which was a signal to Kate that the meeting was over.

"Just remember who gave you the tip," Candy said.

"I will, and Candy, thank you so much for getting the information to us," said Connor.

The news crew pulled its van into the station parking lot as Connor and Kate pulled out. Candy was getting into her car. The cameraman ran across the parking lot.

"Candy, wait. Candy!" He whistled to get her attention.

Candy stopped and lowered her window. "This better be good. I was just leaving to get some dinner before I have to be on the air at six," Candy said.

"The dog, that beagle the Lakewood Police Department is looking for. Come in for a second," the cameraman said, trying to catch his breath.

"You have her?" Candy asked.

"Park your car. I'll have someone pick up your meal. Let me show you this."

Candy raised her window and pulled back into the parking spot with her name on it.

Back in the station, she sat in the darkened editing room, watching footage from the house where the con who'd escaped from jail had tried to pick up his son. Candy watched the unedited news segment and then started getting up from her chair. The cameraman put his large hand on her forearm.

"Wait," he said.

Next came the interview of the Hispanic woman describing, as best she could, how a little puppy had saved her life. The camera faded to black when, suddenly; a small beagle pushed open the screen door and ran down the stairs. The camera rolled as the dog ran to the news van, then looked around at the police cars. The news crew had managed to capture the image of a beagle running from one police car to the next. Not finding anyone in them, the dog took off down the street. In the background, a small boy came from the opposite direction, calling out the name Biscuit. However, the beagle never stopped. The camera swung toward the small boy who was calling out, "Sundae, come back here" before he started to cry.

"That's her, that's Sundae!" Candy said as she got up. "Save the footage!" she called over her shoulder. "I need to call the Lakewood Police Department."

CHAPTER 20

While Connor and Kate waited for word on Dustin Rodney's NCIC check, they went to Julia McCord's home. They hoped Julia could provide a complete list of items that should be in the safety deposit box. They planned to take her to the Lakewood Bank and Trust so she could inventory the box and see what, if anything, had been taken. While at her home, they also wanted her to look at the color photo from Dustin's online social media profile. They wanted to see if she could make a positive ID of Dustin as the man who'd spent time with her husband before his abduction.

Kate pulled up Dustin's social media page on her smartphone so they could show Julia the photo. "I hate going to the McCord home," she said.

"I know," Connor replied. "She always panics, thinking we have bad news about Garrett."

Kate's cell phone rang. Connor's full attention was on the road … until he heard Kate mention Sundae's name.

"What about Sundae?" Connor asked as Kate disconnected the call.

"That was Sandy. A news crew was shooting a segment about a guy who switched ID bracelets with another inmate and got out of jail. The uniforms took the call."

"What does that have to do with Sundae? You said Sundae's name," Connor said impatiently.

"Let me finish. According to the story, the elderly lady's grandson found a little beagle about three days ago and brought her home. This dirtbag forced his way into her house, trying to take his son. He threatened her. Sundae stopped it … or I guess I should say a beagle fitting Sundae's description stopped it. They were finishing up the segment when the beagle pushed open the screen to the front door, then ran down the steps to the news van and the police units parked out front."

"They got her. Thank God!" Connor interrupted. He breathed a sigh of relief.

"Connor, they couldn't get her. But she's on the film. Sandy said that Candy looked at the frames of the beagle and IDed her as Sundae."

Connor's face fell as his excitement turned to distress.

"Connor, at least we know she's alive."

"Call Bob and Grant and see if they have time

to talk to Mrs. McCord. If they do, give them the URL to Dustin's social media profile so they can show Julia the photo."

Connor continued. "Also, we need the ID of the inmate. Was he locked up prior to the Amber Howell murder and the Garrett abduction? Probably a long shot. Next, find out where the grandmother and little boy live. I want to talk to them. Maybe Sundae went back to their house. On the way, we can run by my house to see if she ran back there." Connor pulled over to the side of the road until Kate could get the address where Sundae had last been seen.

Detectives Bob Barton and Grant Harris sat at the kitchen table with Julia McCord. Bob was on his second cup of coffee as Julia listed items as well as cash that had been in the box. Grant took notes.

"So, you believe the box contained at least thirty thousand dollars, all in hundred-dollar bills?" Bob asked.

Julia nodded. "That was money from cattle sales throughout the years. I wanted to put it into CDs or something that earned interest but Garrett insisted that it be put away where we wouldn't spend it."

Grant continued writing down all the information so he could file a report.

"The jewelry belonged to my mother." Julia

chuckled. "I thought it was safer in our safety deposit box. You know, in case someone ever broke in here." She looked down at her hands on the table. "Even with insurance, those things can't be replaced."

"Mrs. McCord, do you have photos of the jewelry, in case it's missing?" Grant asked.

"Actually, I had a jewelry store give us an insurance quote when Mom passed. Our insurance company required us to have a jeweler do an appraisal for the purpose of insuring the items. I have that as well as the photos and descriptions of each piece. I'll go upstairs and get it."

While Julia was upstairs, Bob stood and looked around. On the mantel were photos of Julia and Garrett during various stages of their life together. Next to a recliner stood an oak table that held a phone and a box of tissues. It looked as though the fireplace hadn't been lit since Garrett disappeared. Bob looked at another table that, for some reason, seemed out of place. It held some pens and a few chairs were scattered around it. He assumed this was where the FBI and Lakewood Police had waited for a call demanding a ransom – a call that had never come.

Julia returned with a large tan envelope. Bob quickly sat back down as she opened it and spread the contents on the table. He scanned the jeweler's typewritten letter to the McCord's insurance company, stating the complete collection was worth twenty-five thousand dollars. Bob turned the letter around so Grant could write down the figure.

"Mrs. McCord, this letter was written three years ago. As you know, the price of gold and silver can fluctuate. We may need to see what the jeweler believes the current values are," Bob said.

"I can give him a call tomorrow. I'll go into Garrett's office and make you a copy of all this," Julia said.

"Thank you, that would be helpful. But before you do that, was there anything else in the box that you can remember?" Bob asked.

"We kept our social security cards, our birth certificates, and the titles to his truck and my car in there," Julia said.

Bob glanced at Grant, a concerned look on his face. "Mrs. McCord, I can't finish my report until we meet at the bank tomorrow and determine what was taken from the box. Also, please call the credit bureaus and explain what has happened. Ask them to notify you if anyone attempts to take out a loan or buy anything. In short, they need to call you before any line of credit is issued."

Julia nodded. Bob and Grant stood.

"Mrs. McCord, one more thing before we leave. Can you take a good look at this photo?" Grant held out his cell phone, which showed the social media page of Dustin Rodney. "Is this the man who was with your husband before his abduction?"

Julia put on her glasses and sat on the kitchen chair, staring at the phone.

CHAPTER 21

The living room was tiny and dimly lit. A crucifix hung on the far wall. The house was clean, though it was easy to see a scuffle had taken place, as on a table lay a broken ceramic vase and a cracked family photo.

The old woman motioned for Connor and Kate to take a seat on the plastic-covered furniture. Each time Kate adjusted her position, the plastic against the fabric of her black slacks made a noise. The two detectives sat as the old woman made her way down the hallway with the aid of a cane, calling out to her grandson.

Slowly, Carlos made his way down the darkened hallway. His eyes were red from crying. As he wiped them with his sleeve, he sniffed back more tears.

Connor and Kate stood. "I'm Detective Connor Maxwell and this is my partner, Detective Kate

Stroup," Connor said, shaking the boy's small hand as they all sat down.

"Are you going to … arrest me?" Carlos asked with a shaky voice.

"Arrest you? No. We understand you took in our K9," Connor said.

The boy didn't respond. It was clear he didn't understand what Connor had said.

"Our police dog, Sundae," Connor clarified.

The boy looked up as more tears filled his eyes. "I didn't know she was a police dog, not right away. I found her in the alley. I thought she was hurt or dead. I love doggies. So, I knelt beside her and began to pet her. She woke up. I carried her home." He turned and looked at his grandmother. "Nana said I could keep her if no one said they owned her after a week." More tears rolled down Carlos' cheeks.

Connor looked over and saw a bed, a blanket, some toys, and a food bowl in the corner of the room.

"Have you had a dog before?" Connor asked.

Carlos saw Connor looking over at the dog bed. "No, sir. I always wanted a puppy. I asked Santa for one every year but I never got one. When I found Biscuit, I mean Sundae, I thought my prayers had been answered. When Nana told me I could keep her, I went to the store to buy her food. I told the lady at the store that I wanted a pretty collar, a toy, and a bed. The store owner told me that her dog had gone to heaven and she gave me all her puppy's things. Her puppy's name was Biscuit, so that's what I called her." Carlos looked down as fresh tears welled up and streamed down his cheeks. "I miss her so much."

"Carlos, everyone at the police department misses Sundae, too. So do I, very much. She lives with me. You said you didn't know at first who Sundae was. When did you find out?" Connor asked.

"Yesterday evening. My cartoons stopped on the TV. The news lady showed a picture of Sundae. Sundae was watching cartoons with me, so I asked her if her name was Sundae. Her head came up. She looked like the doggie in the picture on TV. But I wanted a doggie so bad ... and I love her," Carlos said. He paused, then continued. "Nana asked me to hang up papers that said I had found a little doggie. Our phone number was on them. I tossed them in the trash."

"Hito, shame on you," Nana said.

Carlos lowered his head in shame. "I'm sorry, Nana. I just loved her so much," Carlos said.

Connor took a deep breath. He didn't want to hurt the boy. He believed Carlos truly loved Sundae and meant her no harm by his actions. However, Connor also knew that the men and women of the Lakewood Police Department counted on Sundae. He sat for a minute, thinking.

"Tell you what. Will you promise me that if

Sundae comes back here, you'll call me?" Connor asked.

Carlos nodded.

"Carlos, if your grandmother agrees, what would you think if I got you another puppy like Sundae? I'll even try to find a little beagle for you," Connor said.

Carlos' eyes lit up.

"Plus, you can visit Sundae anytime you want at the police station."

Carlos jumped up and down and ran to his grandmother. "Nana, please, can I have a puppy … please?"

The old women smiled at the boy and nodded her approval.

"I never knew you were such a softie," Kate said as Connor pulled the car out of the driveway.

Connor didn't say anything as they drove around looking for Sundae. After about an hour, he dropped off Kate and headed for home.

That evening, Connor opened his front door several times and peered out, hoping and praying Sundae would be there. Each time, he was greeted by only darkness and the emptiness of her absence. He wondered where she could be.

The clock on his nightstand ticked away the seconds as Connor turned over in bed. In his dreams, he heard Sundae howl, then bark. A smile formed on his lips. He heard it again but this time it wasn't a dream.

Connor woke with a start. He heard it again, a howl coming from the front door. He jumped out of bed, wearing only a pair of boxers. Connor stumbled along the dark hallway and unlocked the front door. He peeked out.

There, Sundae sat on the doormat, looking up at him.

Quickly, Connor opened the front door. Sundae trotted into the living room as if nothing had happened.

Connor crouched down. "Hey, young lady, where have you been? Do you know how worried I've been? How worried everybody has been?" he asked.

Sundae crawled into his lap. Connor hugged her.

"I missed you. Boy, do you need a bath!" Connor said as he cradled Sundae in his arms.

He carefully checked Sundae for any cuts or bumps, then held a finger in front of Sundae's eyes, watching as she tracked the finger's movement.

"Looks like you're okay but I'd feel much better if your vet looked you over."

Connor dialed the after-hours number for Sundae's vet. Then he took Sundae right to the vet's office. He felt like a worried parent. After a thorough exam, the vet gave Sundae her blessing to go back to work.

When they were done at the vet, Connor drove to a 24/7 fast food place and picked up two large roast beef sandwiches to go. He knew Sundae loved roast beef.

Once home, Connor opened his sandwich. Then he opened the foil wrapper on Sundae's sandwich and pulled the bread off it. He scraped the beef into Sundae's bowl. Sundae made short work of the food, finishing it long before Connor did.

After they finished, Connor ran some warm bath water. He retrieved towels and Sundae's shampoo and conditioner from the linen closet, using the items to clean up Sundae.

The next morning, Sundae received quite the welcome from the members present at the Lakewood Police Department. Kate grabbed Sundae into her arms and gave her a big hug. Sandy made sure Sundae got some of the treats she kept in her desk.

Detective Bob Barton showed the social media photo of Dustin Rodney to Mrs. McCord. She couldn't rule out Dustin. She said that he looked very much like the man who had been with her husband before the abduction but something was off. She wasn't sure what it was. Hearing this, Connor wondered if it was the fact that Dustin wasn't wearing fancy clothes. It was just a gut feeling. Bob then took the photo to Maggie at the Lakota. She said the same thing; she couldn't rule him out but something was off.

Connor and Kate looked over Dustin's record. While no abduction charges were listed, he'd been arrested for robbery, assault, and selling stolen property. Connor and Kate felt it was time to pay a visit to Dustin. To get the lay of the land, they slowly drove past the old, run-down, single-wide trailer. They saw a door in the front and one in the back.

"You take the back," Connor said. "Take Sundae with you. I'll take the front." They approached the house and took their places. "Dustin Rodney." Connor knocked on the door. "Open up. Police!"

CHAPTER 22

At Dustin's address, the residents either refused to answer or weren't home. Connor tried the doorknob; the door was unlocked. He doubted it would lock, even if someone had wanted it to. The exterior of the knob dangled so far out the door, he could see the exposed wood from the inside. The doorknob mounting plate, with two screws and part of the cylinder, was also exposed. Looking at the door, Connor thought to himself that Dustin sure needed some DIY homeowner tips. Connor listened but couldn't hear anything inside. He carefully opened the door.

"Going inside," he said in a low tone, speaking to Kate through his wrist mic.

Connor cautiously entered the mobile home, his Glock unholstered. One step, listen. Nothing. Another step, turning left to right. Kate and Sundae waited at the back door, knowing Dustin could burst through it at any second.

Connor's eyes hadn't yet fully adjusted from the sunlight outside to the dark interior of the mobile home. The stench was terrible. He noticed that, instead of curtains, aluminum foil was taped to the windows, preventing any sunlight from entering. Dustin – or whoever lived here – had done this to every window in this house, which accounted for the darkness. Connor had seen this done in many places where drug use was prevalent or where a drug lab was present. He wondered if this was where Dustin took his victims.

Connor couldn't imagine how anyone lived like this. The kitchen counter had not one square inch of clear space. Dirty glasses, plates, beer bottles, and half-eaten food in containers were piled high. On the floor lay an open pizza box containing two pieces of pepperoni, which looked to be at least three weeks old. A mouse squeaked, jumped from the pizza box, and ran off down the hallway before disappearing. The trashcan had toppled over, spilling its contents onto the floor. Something caught Connor's attention and he looked down. A cockroach ran over the top of his boot while another scurried into a corner of the room. Connor cleared the living room and kitchen.

Next was a long, dark hallway. Connor used his boot to kick open the door of a small bedroom to his left. He looked around. A stained mattress lay on the floor along with beer bottles, cigarette packs, and food wrappers. The bi-fold closet doors stood against the wall beside the closet. At a glance, Connor could see that the closet contained an odd combination of inkjet paper, rope, duct tape, and questionable magazines. From hangers hung high-dollar suits, shirts, ties, and slacks, all of which seemed very out of place in this house. Beside the bed was a collection of first-aid items including a roll of gauze, a tube of over-the-counter antibiotic cream, medical tape, and a box of four-by-four gauze pads. Connor remembered that Sundae had held onto the perp's ankle.

Every minute Connor was in the trailer, Dustin was looking more and more like their perp. After clearing that room, Connor moved on to the bathroom. The toilet seat was up, exposing a filthy bowl. A razor sat next to the equally dirty sink, where a slimy bar of green soap had slid down. Connor noticed several bottles of aftershave on a shelf over the toilet.

Last was the bedroom at the end of the trailer. Dustin must have used this room as an office. An old, beat-up desk sat in the center of the room. On the desk, a modem blinked, showing connectivity though no computer was present. An expensive printer and a laminating machine sat on the floor.

"Dustin, you're getting more interesting by the minute," Connor said to himself. Then he called out to Kate: "All clear!"

The back door was jammed and couldn't be opened from either the outside or the inside. Kate and Sundae came around and met Connor in the living room. Kate looked around the place.

"Wow, another home taken straight from the pages of Better Homes and Gardens," Kate said. "When we find Dustin, I'll have to ask for the name of his decorator." Kate laughed.

"We have a lot of interesting things in here," Connor said as they walked back to the car. He spoke into the mic: "15, PD. I'd like to request a unit at 4465 Hickory Road. Please give them the photo we have of Dustin Rodney. I want them out of sight and to let me know when he gets back here." Then Connor started the car and pulled away.

"I wonder where he's gone," Kate said.

"He has such a comfy place here, it's hard to imagine he'd want to leave. We need a search warrant for that entire place." Connor told Kate what he'd seen when he was inside looking for Dustin. "On his social media page, did Dustin mention any watering holes he frequents? Any places he goes regularly?"

Kate didn't answer. Instead, she picked up her phone and begin scrolling through Dustin's posts.

"Here's one. Two nights ago, he posted about being at The Snakehole Lounge. From the looks of the post, it's a pretty seedy place," Kate said as she continued scrolling through the posts. "I wish

Candy had gotten the name of the woman who called her. If only we could talk to her."

"Do you think Candy has the name and is withholding it? To do her own thing?" Connor asked.

"I'm not sure," Kate said, giving the question some thought.

Connor drove down Chandler Avenue, turned right on Mountain Road, and headed east. Then he turned left onto Central Avenue. At 1890 Central, he pulled the police unit into The Snakehole Lounge. In the parking lot, a man and a woman were making out in an old, beat-up truck.

Connor and Kate walked into the club. "What can I do you for?" asked the bartender.

Connor looked around. At this hour, the place was empty except for a couple in the far corner. Connor pulled out a printed photo of Dustin and slid it across the bar. "Have you seen this guy in here?"

"Who wants to know?"

Connor took out his badge and ID. "We do."

The bartender thought for a second. "He comes in here every once in a while," the bartender said, wiping down the counter.

"How often is 'every once in a while'?"

"I don't know … I can't remember," replied the bartender.

"Listen. I bet if I call the city authorities, they can shut this place down faster than you can make a

Fireball. Now think real hard." Connor pulled out his phone and acted like he was going to dial a number from his contact list.

"Look, man, he comes in and then you don't see him for weeks. His name is Dustin. That's all I know. He pays his tab and his lady friend's, then leaves."

Connor pressed three keys on his phone. "You serve food on this counter. Funny; I have a photo of a woman lying on it while they did Jell-O shots. Isn't that right, Detective Stroup? Maybe you should pull out that photo and refresh his memory." Connor pressed another key on his phone.

"Okay, okay … one chick did ask me for help. Said Dustin was a real rough guy. Told me she was scared of him. I called her a cab and she left out the back. Dustin got real upset when he found out she'd run out on him," the bartender said.

"Did he or anyone else ever mention where he works?" Connor asked.

"Don't know. Really, I don't. He always has a wad of cash. That's all I know about the dude."

CHAPTER 23

The two unmarked cars parked parallel to each other in the parking lot of the large home improvement store. The cars faced in opposite directions with their drivers' side windows down and across from one another. Kate, Connor, and Sundae sat in one car while Bob and Grant sat in the other. This was customary for law enforcement, as it allowed them to discuss something without tying up the Lakewood Police radio.

Through the windshield, which was as speckled as an Easter egg, Connor looked at the trees skirting both sides and the back of the big box store. He watched as the wind bent the thinner tree trunks and stripped the leaves from their outstretched branches. Some of the trees stood naked in the wind, not a leaf left on them. Cold weather was just around the corner, Connor thought.

There were still no answers in Amber's case.

The Howells had stopped calling each day. As the hands of time ticked away, their calls had gone to every other day and then once a week.

Julia McCord was still calling daily, talking to Kate. Kate was good with families. She was able to handle the emotions much better than Connor was. Garrett's body hadn't been found and Julia never gave up hope.

"We put out the word on the streets. We want any information on Dustin Rodney," Connor said.

"Grant and I have done the same with our snitches. You really think this is our man?" Bob asked.

"Both Maggie at the Lakota and Julia McCord thought he looked like the guy but both felt something was off. Neither could tell me what it was. So, Mr. Dustin Rodney is a person of interest at this time. Honestly, we had no solid leads until this unknown woman called Candy Martian out of the blue. If I could have caught that damn dirtbag at the funeral that day..." Connor shook his head, still frustrated with himself.

"Stop beating yourself up over that," Bob said, knowing that Connor blamed himself for not getting this monster off the street the day of the funeral.

Connor looked out over the hood of their car.

"Hey, did you find a beagle for that little boy yet?" Grant asked, changing the subject.

"Called the lady I adopted Sundae from. She

thinks she may have a lead on one. Good kid; really loves dogs. I think Sundae thought she was on vacation, watching cartoons and sleeping in late. His grandmother has brought him into the PD twice to see Sundae. I think she's Lakewood's own recruitment officer. The boy wants to become a police officer when he grows up." Connor reached over the seat and stroked Sundae's long, soft ears.

"The radio crackled to life. "15."

"15, go ahead PD." Connor waited for dispatch to continue.

"My uniforms just told me your bird has come home to roost."

Dispatch was referring to the plainclothes officers watching Dustin Rodney's place. Sandy used the word "bird" rather than saying Dustin's name in case he had a police scanner. The police were finding that their own radio transmissions were tipping off more and more criminals.

Connor turned the key in the ignition. The engine roared to life.

"Show us en route along with 89 and 92." Connor was stating that Bob and Grant would be assisting them.

Connor weaved in and out of traffic. He wasn't about to let the guy get away this time. Bob and Grant followed closely.

"15, 92, take the back side of the mobile home. Be advised that Kate said the back door was sealed shut. Aluminum foil is on every window, so there's no visual," Connor radioed to Bob.

"10-4," responded Bob.

Fifteen minutes later, Connor pulled up to the two plainclothes officers standing by.

"He went inside about twenty minutes ago. Hasn't come out yet," said one of the officers to Connor.

"Kate and I will take the front." Connor pointed to one of the officers as Bob and Grant got out of their unit. "I need you to go with them."

"PD, be advised that we'll be entering the chicken coop."

"10-4. You all be careful, please."

"You come with us." Connor motioned to the remaining officer.

Slowly and methodically the six officers approached the mobile home, three to the front and three to the rear. Sundae sniffed the dried grass around the house as Connor placed himself on one side of the front door, and then knocked.

"Dustin Rodney, open up! Lakewood Police!" Connor yelled.

They heard footsteps followed by the sound of glass breaking toward the back of the house. Just as Connor entered the house, he saw Dustin jump through the side window. Connor ran out of the house, his feet never touching the stairs as he hit the ground at a dead run.

"He's on the run!" Bob said into his mic.

Sundae followed Connor, who drew a deep breath. He didn't want to give Sundae the order to chase this dirtbag but he knew he had to do it.

"Give chase!" he commanded as he continued following Dustin.

Sundae ran past the plainclothes officer and grabbed Dustin by the ankle just before he reached the wooded area at the back of the house. As Sundae grabbed him, Dustin tripped. Dustin kicked Sundae off his leg, then got to his feet to run. Dried grass and dust flew into the air as Sundae grabbed him once more.

Connor reached for Dustin as he pulled a gun from his belt and aimed it at Connor. Sundae dove at his gun hand. A shot strayed off into the woods. Connor grabbed Dustin's arm and the plainclothes officer pulled the Smith and Weston .38 Special from Dustin's hand. Connor flipped Dustin over on his stomach. Dustin was still resisting arrest as Connor pulled one hand behind his back

Connor pulled his cuffs from his belt and cuffed one of Dustin's hands while the plainclothes officer helped pull Dustin's other arm around until both hands were cuffed behind his back.

Connor pulled Dustin to his feet. "So, this is how you treat your guests? That wasn't very nice of you to run out on us and pull a gun on me."

Dustin said nothing. He spat at Connor, who looked closely at him. Was this the dirtbag whom he'd chased at Amber's funeral?

"All we want to do is have a little chat with you downtown this afternoon. See how you are."

"Screw you, cop!"

"What manners you have. However, now that you pulled that gun on me …"

CHAPTER 24

Dustin Rodney sat in the small room that the detectives called "the box." Drab gray paint covered the bare walls. A single metal table sat next to the far wall, bolted to the floor. Dustin, still combative, sat in a wooden chair. Earlier, in the booking room, Connor had removed Dustin's handcuffs. Dustin had seized the opportunity to lunge at Connor. Bent at the waist, he rammed Connor with the full force of his shoulders, aiming for his gut and ribs. The ink blotter on the table, used for taking prints, became airborne along with a wire tray of blank offense and incident reports. The force knocked the wind out of Connor as he struggled with Dustin. Bob and Grant quickly grabbed Dustin off of Connor, then struggled to put the cuffs back on Dustin. It was clear that Dustin had to remain in cuffs.

Once he was brought into the small

interrogation room, they attached Dustin's cuffs to the metal ring on the table. Connor left the room and walked down the hallway. Still sore, he winced as he touched his rib cage. He rounded the corner and saw Kate coming down the hallway.

"Is Mrs. McCord on her way?" Connor asked.

"She is. I called Maggie. Her manager is giving her time off to come in as well. There's no reason to call the Howells, as they never saw the man before Amber…" Kate stopped herself before she said any more. She turned and started to walk away, then turned back to Connor and looked at him closely. "You okay?

"Just a little issue with Dustin in the booking room," Connor said. "I'm fine."

"Connor, shouldn't Sundae have expressed more interest in Dustin than she did? After all, we assumed that he hit her on the side of the head where her vet found the lump. She chased him through the cemetery and out into the streets that day."

Connor looked down at Sundae, who was sitting next to his left leg. The muscles in his jaw flexed as he reflected on Kate's question.

"I thought about that back at his trailer," he replied. "It appeared as though she was just following my orders for a takedown. Maybe it was the lack of aftershave. I didn't smell any on him today."

A uniformed officer led Julia McCord toward

them. Julia extended her arms and gave Kate a hug. After the embrace, Connor walked the women back toward the box and the one-way glass.

"Julia, we have a suspect in this room. He can't hear or see you, so please don't worry," Connor said.

Julia stepped forward and peered into the glass. She stared at Dustin. The three watched him as he pulled the handcuffs in a see-saw motion, trying to free himself. His face and neck were red with anger.

"He's like an animal," Julia said. She shuddered, as though a shiver had run up her spine.

"But is he the man who was at your house with your husband?" asked Kate.

"He certainly didn't dress that way when he was at the house. Honestly, I tried to ignore him most of the time. Can you ask him to say, 'Is Garrett home?' Maybe I can recognize his voice."

Connor realized that Julia was trying to recognize a speech pattern. He walked over, punched a code into the door lock, and walked into the box. Then he calmly walked around to face Dustin, careful to avoid blocking the sight from the window.

"Dustin, have you calmed down?"

Dustin said nothing. Instead, he continued to jerk the cuffs back and forth. He also spat at Connor. The veins in his neck, forehead, and forearms bulged as he strained to get loose.

"Police brutality," he said, holding up his cuffed hands.

"Dustin, I really need you to calm down."

Dustin continued to jerk his arms back and forth until blood appeared around his wrists. He didn't seem to notice it.

Connor looked up at the red dots of the cameras, which were recording from the four corners of the room. "I have a favor to ask." Connor stood and waited for a reply.

"Screw you, cop!"

"Actually, I was going to ask you to say, 'Is Garrett home?'"

Dustin stopped pulling on the cuffs and looked wide-eyed at Connor. "Who the hell is Garrett?"

Connor figured that was all he was going to get out of Dustin. Nevertheless, he asked one more time. Still, Dustin refused to say anything. Connor walked out of the room and pulled the door shut.

"I want an attorney. I know you can hear me."

"Mrs. McCord, he's refusing to cooperate," Connor said. "When he said your husband's name, did it sound familiar?" Connor looked at Julia, then at the uniformed officer approaching them.

"I think so." A tear ran down her cheek. "I'm just not sure."

"Detective Maxwell, we have Mr. Rodney's report," the officer said. "He's been through the revolving door of the system since he was sixteen years old. Started with petty theft, armed robbery, and possession of a controlled substance, then moved on to assault, stalking, and forgery. You can see for yourself, Detective." The uniformed officer handed the reports to Connor.

Connor glanced over the reports. Kate escorted Julia McCord into another room. Several minutes later, Maggie was escorted down the same hallway.

"Detective," Maggie said, looking Connor over and flashing a flirtatious smile at him.

"Maggie, how are you doing?" Connor asked.

"Fine. Detective Stroup asked if I could come over and take a look at someone."

"We have a suspect we want you to look at, to see if you recognize him," Connor said. He led her to the glass.

"Can he see me?" Maggie asked as she stepped away from it.

"No, not at all. It's one-way. You can see and hear him," Connor said.

Dustin seemed to be trying to use every cuss word he'd ever heard in his life.

"He does look like the guy from the restaurant, but he's definitely not dressed like him," Maggie said. "Does he smell like he took a bath in his aftershave? He always wore an expensive wristwatch, too. A Rolex, I think."

"No, not a scent of aftershave on him. Not today, anyway. Nor did he dress for the occasion, as you can see. Guess he didn't want to impress me," Connor said.

Maggie furrowed her brow and looked again at the man in the box.

"Maggie, we'll need you to write out a statement," Connor said. He walked her down the hall to another room.

CHAPTER 25

Dustin was booked into the county jail for eluding and assault of a peace officer, possession of a controlled substance, and felon in possession of a firearm. The detectives felt confident that they had enough to hold him.

They didn't want to bring formal charges against him for the murder of Amber Howell and the disappearance of Garrett McCord. At this point, he was still a person of interest. Connor had an inmate moved into the cell next to Dustin's. Connor knew that this inmate would provide valuable information ... *if* Dustin would open up and talk to him.

It was Tuesday afternoon, three days after Dustin Rodney had been arrested on a cocktail of charges.

The sun made a futile attempt to warm up the day; however, the end result was only 58 degrees, and chillier in the higher elevations.

Avery Fletcher and his wife, Gabby, were walking on the trail that led up to Taylor Peak. With them was their Jack Russell Terrier, Jinx. Avery had been working fifty hours per week and Gabby had asked for some "us" time. The two of them had gone to visit both of their parents in a nearby town. They had also gone out to dinner every night so that Gabby didn't have to cook and clean up afterward. They slept in late and decided to spend the last three days of their vacation camping at Taylor Peak. On their last night, they snuggled in a warm blanket near the campfire. The next morning, they decided to explore a trail they hadn't been on before. Hand in hand, they walked up the trail, talking about their time off and their dreams of someday owning a house. Jinx scampered ahead, enjoying the new smells. Suddenly, he ran off the trail and disappeared into the tall brush.

"Jinx, come!" Gabby called to the small Jack Russell.

Jinx refused to come. He began barking loudly.

"I'll check on him. He probably cornered a rabbit," Avery said. He walked down into the thicket. Pulling back the branches, he saw Jinx barking at something lying under the thick brush.

"Come on, you little …" Avery stopped. As he

bent down to pick up the dog, he saw a man's arm sticking out from under a pile of leaves.

"Holy… sh …"

Avery was stopped mid-sentence by his wife, who walked up behind him. "Was it a rabbit?" Gabby asked.

Avery turned sideways and pointed at the arm.

My God, what happened?" Gabby asked.

"I don't know."

"Is he alive?" Gabby asked.

Avery bent down and felt the cold wrist. There was no pulse. He shook his head. "Do we have any cell service?"

Gabby quickly pulled her phone from her back pocket. "No. Is all the body there or just that arm?" she asked. "God, this gives me the creeps!"

Avery pulled back the branches and peeked over. "Yes, it's all there, but no clothes. He has black marks all over him."

"Let's go down the trail where we can get a signal and call the police."

Avery thought for a second. He pulled off his jacket, then his flannel shirt, and finally his t-shirt. "I'll mark the area with my t-shirt on this branch."

The couple quickly left the area.

"I wonder what could've happened to him," Gabby said.

"His face is all bruised and cut up. I'd say he fell from one of the cliffs, but that area wasn't bad. Maybe animals dragged him there. However, that doesn't make sense, with him not having any clothes on."

"I have a signal now," Gabby said. She handed her phone to Avery.

The sheriff's department arrived in about forty-five minutes.

Connor and Kate received the call from Detective Kraft at the Natick Sherriff's Department and arrived on the scene. The ME was already there when Connor and Kate hiked up the trail with Sundae sniffing along the way. Connor bent over the body and squatted down for a closer look.

"That's Garrett McCord," he said to Detective Kraft.

"I thought so from the photos. Looks like he was tortured before he was killed and the body dumped here," Kraft said.

Connor stood and listened for Sundae. He wanted to see if she picked up on anything. She quickly ran back to Connor's side.

"How long has the body been out here?" Connor asked the ME.

"This body has been out here for maybe a week, tops," Malcolm Greenblat said. "The cold weather out here helped preserve it. I can tell you that he suffered repeated beatings before he died. There are bruises on his back, rib area, and legs, as well." Malcolm lifted the torso to one side.

"But the cause of death was strangulation," he continued. "I would make an educated guess that it was another Mexican bow tie. See where the barbs dug in along the line on his throat?" Malcolm looked at Connor.

Kate finished taking the Fletchers' statement as to how they'd found the body. They stayed until the body was taken by gurney down the trail and loaded into the ME's van. The next step in the process was one of the hardest: breaking the news to Julia McCord, who had held out hope that her husband was still alive. Connor wondered if Julia would be able to go down to the ME's office to make a positive ID.

They pulled the unit up the long driveway to the ranch house. Julia must have seen them coming, as she was standing on the porch. When Connor and Kate stepped out of the car, Julia looked at their faces. Before they could say anything, she fell to her knees.

No, please, no!" she cried out.

Kate ran to her side and held her.

CHAPTER 26

The Texas state trooper had been sitting between the eastbound and westbound lanes on the I-40 median for the last forty-five minutes. He was pointing his radar gun in the direction of the eastbound traffic. Finn McClain had been with the department for the last five years and he knew that when things got slow, he could use the time to catch up on reports. He polished off a cup of coffee as he finished the last report. Then he stacked them neatly back into the metal case on his front seat.

Finn was gazing out over the hood of his state-issued SUV when he saw a Chevy Silverado heading east at a high rate of speed. As the truck approached, the radar gun emitted an audible warning. Finn glanced down at the digital readout on the radar gun, which flashed ninety-two miles per hour. Finn engaged his lights and siren in pursuit of the truck, which slowly pulled over onto the shoulder of the highway.

"Do you know why I pulled you over?" Finn asked the driver of the truck.

"No, officer, I don't."

Finn thought to himself, 'God, how I wish I had a dime for every time someone said that. I could easily retire early.'

"You were going ninety-two. The posted speed limit is seventy-five on this stretch of I-40," Finn said. "License and registration, please."

Finn looked the driver over carefully and judged him to be in his early thirties. The driver pulled out his wallet.

"Please remove the license from your wallet," Finn requested.

The driver complied, then handed the license to the trooper. Finn didn't look at the license he now held in his hand. Rather, he kept a close eye on the driver as he retrieved the registration from the glove box and handed it to the trooper.

Finn stepped back to his patrol car and ran the plate and license through his onboard computer. He looked once, then blinked his eyes. 'It's been a long day,' he thought to himself. He looked again, then once more. The VIN attached to the license plate was for a vehicle wanted by the Lakewood Police Department in connection with a murder. Finn felt his heart beating as he looked at the plate and glanced out his windshield at the truck for a second time. The license plate attached to the rear bumper didn't match the truck that the Lakewood Police Department was looking for. However, the VIN and the description were a match.

Finn radioed dispatch for backup and was told that the ETA for the nearest officer was twenty minutes at best. Slowly, he got out of his patrol unit and unsnapped his holster. With his SUV door to shield him, he unholstered his weapon and trained it toward the driver-side door. He used his mic and PA system.

"Step out of the truck with your hands on your head. Interlace your fingers."

Finn watched the Chevy's driver-side door open slowly. The male occupant stepped out with his hands on his head.

"On your knees," commanded Finn.

The male subject did as instructed. Finn slowly approached the man and holstered his weapon. He pulled out his handcuffs and placed them on the man's wrists, behind his back. Pulling the man to his feet, Finn patted him down. In the man's jeans, Finn found a large pocketknife. As he pulled it out, Finn felt his own heart still racing.

"Is this your truck?" Finn asked, turning the man around to face him.

"Yes, sir."

"You live in Lakewood?"

"No, sir. I live outside of Amarillo, Texas. My

dad has a ranch there," the young man answered with a shaky voice.

"How long have you had the truck?" Finn asked as his backup rolled to a stop beside his unit.

"I've had it for a little over four weeks. Why? Is something wrong, officer?"

"That's what we have to find out," Finn said as the backup trooper walked toward them.

"You check the truck yet, Finn?" the backup trooper asked.

"Not yet," Finn responded.

"You won't find any booze in there. I don't drink," said the young man as he watched the second officer searching his truck.

Finn pulled the man toward his patrol unit and opened the back door. He put his hand on the young man's head and asked him to sit in the backseat.

"Officer, what's this all about?"

"This truck is wanted in connection to a murder."

"Mur…" The young man couldn't finish, as if the word had caught in his throat. "We bought the truck at an auction. Really. My dad paid cash for it."

"Do you have the title?" Finn asked.

"My dad has it."

"We'll need to see the title," Finn said as he started up the SUV and headed for the county jail.

Finn called the Lakewood Police Department

with the listed contact number while the Texas state detectives questioned the driver of the truck.

The four detectives, along with Beth Ellis, sat in the small situation room to discuss the Howell and McCord cases.

"We know these two cases are linked," Connor said. "Beth, do you have anything more for us?"

"We know the perp is motivated by money. Also, he has absolutely no remorse for his killings."

"Why do you say that?" Bob asked.

"He left Amber Howell's body lying naked and unburied. The same was true for Garrett McCord. When a killer buries a body, we know that's a sign of remorse, or at least some remorse, for his actions."

Beth continued as she looked down at her notes. "Neither victim was sexually assaulted. He used them to get to their money – or, in Amber Howell's situation, he used her father's money. I feel like he must've known that she carried her dad's credit card with a much higher credit limit.

"In the McCord case, he also used the victim's credit cards. We now know that he used the title to McCord's truck to sell the truck, which netted him a little over twenty thousand. He got cash out of the McCords' safety deposit box, approximately thirty thousand. He pawned heirlooms from the safety deposit box, which got him another forty thousand.

Connor told me that Kate learned that a few of Amber's father's clients have had credit established which they didn't apply for. He got that information from the paperwork Amber was carrying with her the morning of the abduction. Therefore, it's safe to conclude that this person is driven by money."

"The method by which he chooses to kill them…"

Beth interrupted Connor.

"The Mexican bow tie. That does throw me off," Beth said, deep in thought. "That, as you know, is his signature. He wants you to know it's him. However, the Mexican mafia usually uses this method. The killer likes to sit on the victim and watch the slow, painful death. The barbs pierce the neck. That's the first thing many killers whom I've interviewed do. The reason they do this is to get more information out of the victim. They let up on the barbs, then apply more pressure if the victim doesn't respond. Most killers I've interviewed select these methods when they're angry with their victim. This makes more sense in the case of the mafia than it does with these victims.

"Beth, we've checked both victims and their families. Neither have ties to the Mexican mafia," Connor said.

"Dustin Rodney had a lucrative business providing fake IDs to people," Bob said. "I looked over his computer and printer as well as a laminating machine. But no connection to the mafia."

"The DA set bond for the other charges against Dustin, but feels that we don't have enough evidence to charge him for the two murders," Kate said.

"Honestly, he just doesn't fit my profile. I believe the person has rich taste, an extravagant house, and a luxury car. This person has expensive clothes and jewelry, eats at only the best restaurants. Dustin Rodney has a few expensive suits, based on what you found in his home closet, but other than that, I don't see the connection.

"We're still keeping a close eye on him since his release," Connor said.

"I understand. Nonetheless, the person you're looking for doesn't live in Lakewood. I believe this type of perp is one who lives outside of his kill zone, which as we now know is Lakewood," Beth said.

"Do you believe he's done this in other areas?" Kate asked.

"He probably has and he'll move if he feels we're getting too close to him. Remember, he's driven by money and needs to keep the cash flowing. He attacks his victims in much the same way that we each go to work every day. To him, the victims, doing research on them, and stalking them is just another day at the office," Beth said.

He sat in his four-star hotel room, reading the front page of the newspaper. The article of interest had Dustin Rodney's photo attached to it.

"While they're busy watching you, I'll be busy with my next," the man said as he set down the newspaper. He picked up his Rolex, admired it, and put it on.

CHAPTER 27

Kristen heard a car coming up the long, well-maintained driveway. She had just gotten home from Jefferson Grade School, where she taught second grade. Kristen was a third-generation educator; both her mother and grandmother had taught school. She loved her job and enjoyed working with children. Kristen felt like she was playing an integral role in modeling the next generation of doctors, lawyers, teachers, and maybe even a president someday. She wanted children of her own. At age twenty-six, she heard her biological clock ticking, as they say. However, for some reason, Jared avoided the subject whenever she brought it up. They had been married only three years this September; there was still time, she reassured herself. She had faith that someday she would be able to convince him.

Kristen stopped in the foyer to look in the

mirror on the wall. She ran her slender fingers through her long brown hair. Jared expected her to always look "presentable," as he called it. Men still did second takes when she walked by. Kristen straightened her blouse, then ran to the front door and opened it.

Jared was coming up the walkway, his oversized duffle bag in his right hand and his locked briefcase in the other. She knew not to ask where he'd been for the last few months. When they were dating, he'd told her that he was an agent with a special division of the FBI and that he could never divulge information about his job or the cases to which he was assigned. However, Kristen still worried when he was gone.

He met her at the door and they embraced. Jared stood back, appraising her, then bent down without a word, picked up his duffle bag and briefcase, and set them in the foyer. He stood there for a few minutes, admiring his house. He had paid a little over six hundred thousand for it in a down market. Today, with housing prices skyrocketing, it was worth much more. The finest furnishings adorned the house, which had been decorated by Colette Cordonnier, a woman who put Martha Stewart to shame, he loved to tell guests. Colette was renowned for her ability to make a house look like it had come right from a page of *House Beautiful* or any of those other glossy magazines. Each room –

including the three bathrooms – had Colette Cordonnier's touch.

When she met Jared, Kristen had wanted to decorate the home or at least add a few of her own personal touches to it. However, Jared had insisted on hiring a professional. After all, what did a schoolteacher he'd met on a dating site know about decorating?

"Do you want to go out for dinner tonight? I didn't know you were coming home or I would've had dinner ready for you," Kristen said.

"No, let's just eat here. I'm going to take a shower. I'll be done in fifteen minutes," Jared said.

He picked up his duffle and briefcase and went upstairs. Once in their bedroom, he pulled his dirty clothes out of the duffle bag and tossed them in the hamper. Then he tossed the empty duffle bag on the closet floor. Jared left his briefcase next to his side of the bed. After all, it was locked, he thought to himself. He stripped naked and headed for the shower. He loved being back home. The hotels he'd stayed at paled in comparison to his gold-plated, thermostatically controlled, six-spray shower made of Italian marble.

He thought of the psychologist to whom he'd been sent when he was a teenager. She'd told his parents he was obsessive-compulsive about material things. The more he had, the more he wanted. Shortly after that, his father had suddenly passed away.

The warm water invigorated him as he washed away the thoughts of his past and the last three weeks of his life. After shutting off the water, Jared grabbed a towel from the towel bar and wrapped it around his waist. He lathered shaving cream on his face and drew his razor downward from his sideburn.

"My God, what happened to your ankle?" Kristen asked, looking down at his ankle, which was still swollen and red and bore several visible puncture wounds.

"Nothing, just part of the job. Some dirtbag tried to slam a door on my leg."

"But…" Kristen reached down toward the wound. "There are puncture marks."

Jared pulled away from his wife.

"I really think you need to see a doctor, honey. That looks infected."

Jared ignored her comment and finished shaving. He put antiseptic cream on his ankle, which he then wrapped with gauze. 'Damn fleabag,' he thought as he flinched in pain, remembering his encounter with that police mutt.

"So, what's for dinner?" he asked, changing the subject and his mood almost as quickly as the blink of an eye. He pulled on a pair of PJ lounging pants and a t-shirt.

"I ordered us a pizza. It should be here in about twenty minutes."

Kristen left the room and headed downstairs.

Jared returned to the bathroom, picked up a three-ounce bottle of Creed aftershave and splashed some on his face. It was one of the many indulgences with which he pleasured himself. The aftershave cost over three hundred dollars a bottle, but Jared always told himself he was worth it. He looked at his reflection in the mirror, and then turned to look at the muscles rippling through the white t-shirt. He ran a comb through his thick hair, getting every hair in place. He liked his own reflection and smiled.

Jared left the bedroom and carried his briefcase directly to his home office. He fished around for the hidden key and unlocked the door. The room was dark. He flipped on the overhead light, then closed the door and locked it behind him. He booted up his computer and searched for any news about the shooting after Amber's funeral, Garrett McCord's body, and his uncle. Next, he checked the dating site for any new interest in his profile. After all, some of his best victims were women interested in dating him. He perused the interested females' profiles, looking for any indication that they or their families had money and that there was an open doorway to the money.

Next, he turned his attention to his briefcase. Jared pulled out a folder he had taken from Amber Howell as well as all the documentation from the McCord's safety deposit box. The folder was worn from use, but he was interested only in what was inside. In talking to Amber, he'd learned that she worked nights from home helping her dad with the books for his CPA firm. Jared would spend the next few months extracting any information he could from the file to form new identities, create new accounts, and move around their money to suit his needs. He smiled, thinking about how easy it would be. He had all the right electronic tools to commit such crimes without a trace.

The doorbell rang; the pizza was early. Jared cleared out his computer browser and left the office, relocking the door behind him. As he came down the stairs, he saw that Kristen had turned on the TV in the great room. He looked over at the ninety-inch flat-screen TV that hung on the wall. There was probably nothing to worry about, with them living one state over from the crimes. Nevertheless, after descending the stairs, he reached for the remote and changed the channel to a twenty-four-hour sports channel. He and Kristen never agreed on the TV channel selection, so he knew that she would switch it off the first chance she got.

CHAPTER 28

It had been three months since he'd killed Amber Howell, a little less than that since Garrett McCord. McCord had turned out to be a real cash cow. With the title to his new truck, cash in the safety deposit box, jewelry, and credit cards, he'd netted a little over a hundred thousand off McCord. He sat thinking about how the redneck had begged for his life, promising to give him everything he wanted and more if he would just let him go home to his wife. When his begging stopped, Garrett had fought him every chance he could, but the redneck was no match for the restraints. He remembered when he'd found the safety deposit box key and asked McCord what bank and what branch the box was in. McCord had refused to answer his questions.

"You'll never live long enough to see or enjoy anything in that safety deposit box of yours anyway." He'd smiled as he'd punched McCord in the gut. When that hadn't resulted in the answer to his questions, he'd removed his shoes and used his kickboxing experience to deliver a brutal kick to McCord's ribs. He'd smiled when he'd heard bones crack.

"Now tell me what bank and which branch."

McCord had winced from the pain in his ribs. The man swung around once more, this time his kick going for McCord's gut.

"Please … no more," McCord had begged.

"Answer my question!"

"My wife opened the box. I have no idea. Really."

With that, the man had spun around on his left foot. The kick punch had hit the other side of McCord's rib cage.

"You're a coward," McCord had said once his breath had returned.

The man had taken out his cell phone and clicked the timer on his phone.

"Every five minutes, I'll help you remember where the bank is with another kick. Every five minutes, I pick another body part until you tell me where the safety deposit box is. Every five minutes … oh, look." He'd pointed at his phone. "You have only three minutes and five seconds left." He'd chuckled.

Sweat had poured from McCord's forehead.

"By you not telling me where the box is pretty

much tells me that something very important is in there."

The man had stood up and taken practice kicks; they hadn't connected with McCord but McCord had flinched each time a foot neared him. When the alarm on his phone had gone off, the man had stepped in front of McCord.

"Well … can you help me find the safety deposit box?"

"I can take you to it. That's the only way."

"Wrong answer!" The man had swung around and kicked McCord's right thigh so hard, it seemed to have broken his femur.

McCord had transferred his weight to his left leg as he watched the man set the timer once again.

"Garrett, Garrett. Certainly, you don't think I'm that stupid, do you? Fact is, that answer should've gotten you a bonus kick." The man had chuckled and spun around, practicing his kicks. Each time, he'd moved closer to McCord's left leg.

"If you'd answer my question, I'll get you a stool to sit on while I go to the bank. That right leg looks pretty swollen. Now, the deal is, if you lie to me and I drive somewhere and the box is not at that bank, you'll wish I had killed you. Understood?"

"Why don't you just kill me now?" McCord had asked.

"Simple. You're still worth something to me alive." The timer had sounded again. Standing in

front of McCord, the man had demanded,
"tell me!"

The door to the metal building had opened and
a man in his fifties had appeared. His mouth had
fallen open when he'd seen his nephew standing in
front of a man chained to the wall.

"Uncle, I thought you weren't supposed to be
back until next week."

"For God's sake, Jared, what the hell are you
doing?"

"Help me, please!" McCord had pleaded to the
older man. "He's a mad man."

"Uncle, let me explain," Jared had said as he
firmly took his arm and escorted his uncle out of
the building.

As Jared drove down Highway 10, he kept thinking
about the events of the past few months. He wished
he didn't have to kill them. The killing was simply
the means to an end. For him, it had always been
that way. He'd prefer to get their money without
killing them, but he knew all too well that this would
lead to his arrest. However, killing his own uncle
bothered him. He reasoned to himself that it was
simply collateral damage. He loved his uncle, who
had taken him under his wing after his father was
killed.

Nevertheless, when his uncle had returned early

from his business trip and found McCord bound with chains, he simply had no choice. Besides, he reasoned, he was the beneficiary of a large life insurance policy that his uncle had left him. It was a shame he'd walked in that day, he thought to himself.

However, his last kill thrilled him, when Garrett begged for his life and then fought him. What was it? Could he be getting used to this? Was it the power he felt over these people?

He wouldn't even have to do this if his own father hadn't been killed. His father was a man of means; growing up, he had never wanted for anything. That is, until they'd taken away his father. They'd taken money from his father, his mother, and him. Added to that was the embarrassment when his father was found naked, a piece of barbed wire with two wooden dowel handles still wrapped around his neck. He'd asked his mother why Papa didn't have his clothes on when he was found. She'd told him that they did this to embarrass the loved ones left behind. It took years for him to truly understand.

He shook his head to clear his thoughts of the past. Now he had to concentrate on his next victim. He pulled his rental car from the road along side the ditch where he had left Amber Howell's body. How long had he sat there thinking? A minute, an hour? Had anyone seen him?

CHAPTER 29

His appointment at Smiles Dental was scheduled for 3:30. Jared glanced down at the Rolex on his wrist. The gold bevel glimmered in the sunlight. He was late. Too much musing back at the ditch where he'd dumped Amber Howell's body months ago. He got out of the rented Lexus and hurried toward the front door of the office. As he caught a glimpse of himself in the reflection in the glass, he straightened his tie and ran his hand through his hair. Then he smiled at his own reflection.

A door chime announced his arrival. He walked to the counter and signed in on the clipboard with the fictitious name of James Lincoln. After taking his seat in the empty lobby, he peered toward the exam rooms. Mia Gordon came out of one and glanced his way with a warm smile.

"We'll be with you in about five minutes," Mia said. She went into the next exam room.

Mia was a well-educated, beautiful, blonde-haired, blue-eyed woman with a perfect figure. She was twenty-something, he figured. Jared had met her at a big box electronics store. She was looking for a new smartphone and he was looking for his next victim.

They'd struck up a conversation while she waited for the salesman to finish up with a customer. Jared flirted with her and talked about his travels. Some of the tales were true, while others were fictional. His stories seemed to interest her, and he made sure to flash his Rolex. He learned that she was not only a dental assistant but also the daughter of the dentist who owned Smiles Dental.

After their meeting, Jared kept busy researching Mia and her father. Dr. Alistair Gordon, whose friends called him Al, owned several successful Smiles Dental offices in and around Lakewood. There certainly seemed to be enough money there. A few days passed before he made an appointment at Smiles.

Mia remembered the handsome, dark-haired, well-traveled man she'd met while buying her new phone. When she walked into the exam room before the dentist – her father – came in, Jared turned on the charm. He convinced her to have dinner and drinks with him one night soon.

Later that week, Mia met him at the restaurant,

where they had dinner and drinks and then danced to slow ballads. Several days later, he called and asked her out to a show she had mentioned wanting to see. When she agreed, his next problem was to get tickets to a popular sold-out show. For most people, this would be impossible, but not Jared. He had tickets in hand within hours. When he met Mia for lunch, he gave her the tickets.

"How?" she asked, unbelieving.

Jared just smiled.

Each time they were together, he gleaned more information about her and her very wealthy father. When asked about her mother, Mia told him that she had been a cardiovascular surgeon and had died in a car accident, leaving large sums of money to her only daughter, Mia, and her husband.

During one of his office visits, he told the receptionist that he had bad pain in a molar, which was untrue, but he wanted to see Mia again. During that office visit, he managed to score a bottle of ether. He also invited Mia to join him for dinner the following Friday night.

Jared started following Mia without her knowledge. Now he knew where she lived, where she shopped, where she had her hair done, and where she banked. Every Thursday, she went to a spa for a massage. Yoga classes were on Tuesday afternoons. She and her father also offered free dental services at a local homeless shelter.

After their fourth date, Mia invited Jared to

spend the night. While she was in the shower, he looked through her purse and quickly gathered checking account and credit card information. He then looked through a file cabinet in her small home office.

The following day, Jared sat in his hotel room with a pen and pad, planning out the details. It was all in the planning; he told himself that was why he was so successful at what he did without getting caught.

The next day, he went to a jewelry shop and purchased an engagement ring. That night, he and Mia dined by candlelight. After a few drinks, Jared felt the time was right. He dropped to one knee.

"Mia, I know we haven't been dating that long, but would you marry me?"

Mia lifted her hands to her face. A tear escaped from the corner of her eye and ran down her cheek.

"I know it's been only a few weeks, but I love you. We can wait to set a date later if that makes you feel better," Jared said, opening the ring box.

"Yes, James Arthur Lincoln, yes!" she said. Her hand trembled as she held it out to him. He placed the ring on her finger.

He smiled. "You don't know how happy you've just made me."

The next day, after leaving Mia's house, he went back to the hotel, where he wasted no time putting the finishing touches on his plan. Jared had no intentions of marrying Mia. Instead, he needed to get as much information as he could about the family business – and, more so, the family money. He knew all too well that a family such as the Gordons had treasures.

However, while Mia became closer and closer to Jared (or James, as she knew him), Dr. Gordon became concerned about his only daughter promising to marry a man she had known for only a few weeks. After all, he'd been a single parent since her mother, his wife, had passed away when Mia was only four years old. His protective nature began to spark fights over her engagement. Mia didn't let this bother her. She thought that, with time, her father would accept James. However, the more Mia and her father fought about James, the more Dr. Gordon worried. Both he and Mia were quite wealthy. What if this man was interested in her only for her money?

After Mia had left the office one evening, Dr. Gordon called a friend who put him in touch with a private investigator who could look into Mr. James Arthur Lincoln. However, he did so without Mia's knowledge. Dr. Gordon told himself that if this man was on the up and up, he would have to respect his daughter's wishes.

CHAPTER 30

J ared dialed his home phone number. After the third ring, he heard the soft voice of his wife, Kristen. He smiled to himself for a second; a wife and a fiancée.

"Hello," Kirsten said.

"Kristen, I'm still out of the country, but I've been calling my uncle for days with no answer. Could you please call the police and have them check on him?"

"Jared, when are you supposed to be coming home?" Kristen asked.

"I hope to have this wrapped up in a month. Can you please check on my uncle? This isn't like him," Jared said.

He knew full well that his uncle was dead. However, the authorities would have to find him dead in order for Jared to collect on the life insurance.

He knew that he couldn't report his uncle missing. His face had been splashed all over the news too many times. Even with the hair dye and beard, as well as the face job he'd had done, he didn't want to take any chances. Let his wife, Kristen, do his dirty work for him. She would report it and, once they found the body, she could ID it. That meant he would soon benefit from the life insurance policy while safely staying out of things.

After he'd killed McCord and his uncle, he'd made sure to clean up, carefully power washing the concrete floors. The best part, he thought to himself, was finding out where Dustin Rodney lived and stealing a few items from Dustin's rathole of a house. He'd then left them in his uncle's shop for the police to find. He chuckled to himself, thinking about the cops chasing their tails.

Kate and Connor looked over the scene where a man around age fifty was found dead by two cyclists on their morning bike ride.

"He wasn't killed here, just dumped. You can see how the blood has settled in the body," Connor said. He looked around for more clues.

"Do you think this is one of "HIS" killings?" Kate asked.

"He was strangled but the bruising around the neck appears to have been done with bare hands.

No Mexican bow tie on this one. Maybe the ME can get some DNA off the body."

Connor walked around, looking for clues. Tire tracks led off the same way they'd driven in.

"We need to see if the tire cast matches any of the others."

Sundae busied herself searching the field. Then she came back to the body. She sniffed the neck of the dead man, sat down, and howled. Connor walked over. He noticed that Sundae was most interested in the bruising where they could clearly make out handprints around the neck. Connor looked over at Kate.

"It seems she thinks this one's a match."

"But there's no Mexican bow tie and this body is clothed," said Kate.

"Maybe he was in a hurry with this one, getting sloppy. They still have the tail on Dustin Rodney. Call the PD. Ask them if he managed to slip the tail at any time."

"There's no ID on the body; just another John Doe unless someone calls in a missing person. Looks like he's been out here for a few days," Kate said.

"Have Sandy check any missing person reports."

Connor looked up as the ME's van rattled down the field toward them. Connor motioned him to come around a different way so as not to disturb the tire imprints for the CSI teams that had been called out.

"A missing person was reported in the county.

Maybe this is our John Doe," Kate said. "County is on the way over to check it out."

Brady Coulter had retired from the Natick County Sherriff's Office and opened his own private investigation firm. He was only fifty-nine years old and loved police work, but hated the politics that sometimes went along with the job at the sheriff's department. He was a one-man show, as he liked to say. This way, things were done the way he liked them. For the most part, he did background checks for companies in the area. He did a few trails on husbands and wives who'd "slipped their leashes" – his way of referring to a cheating spouse. He'd also done a few missing persons cases.

He was reading the morning paper while waiting for his 2:00 appointment to show up. When he'd called, Dr. Al Gordon had asked to meet at Brady's rather than at his dental office. Brady assumed the doctor wanted some employee background checks.

At 1:58, the door opened and Dr. Gordon stepped inside. Brady noticed a faint smell that wafted in with him. Was it antiseptic? Ether? He wondered if all dentists smelled that way.

"You must be Dr. Gordon," Brady said. The two men shook hands. "Sit down. Please tell me, what can I do for you?"

Dr. Gordon sat down and put a file folder on Brady's desk. Brady opened the folder and thumbed through photos of a young woman with a man who looked about fifteen years her senior.

"That's my daughter." Al pointed at the woman in one of the photos.

"Beautiful young lady," Brady said. "And the man is?"

"That's why I'm here," Dr. Gordon said with a heavy sigh. He leaned back in the chair.

Brady noticed the doctor's expression change as he searched for the right words. A long time ago, Brady had learned to never press when talking to someone. He waited and observed the doctor.

"I want to know everything about this man." Dr. Gordon pulled a photo of James from the file.

Do you have a name?" Brady asked

"James Arthur Lincoln," Al Gordon said.

Brady wrote down the information on a pad.

"I'm willing to pay you whatever you need to find out everything you can about this man." Dr. Gordon pulled a small piece of paper from his shirt pocket. "That's the license plate number of the vehicle he drives."

CHAPTER 31

Kristen Hobbs held a tissue in her shaking hands. Her eyes were red and swollen from crying. The county coroner led her to a room with several metal tables. Large round lights hung over them. He walked her over to a table on which rested a body covered with a white sheet. As they approached, Kristen noticed a toe tag labeled "John Doe," along with the date on which the body was found. Kristen stood next to the table as the coroner pulled back the sheet to reveal the body.

"My God. No!" Kristen cried.

"You mentioned he had a tattoo of a dove and a heart on his forearm." The coroner pointed at the tattoo.

Kristen turned her head away from the body.

"Mrs. Hobbs, is this your husband's uncle?" The coroner gently put his arm around her shoulders as her whole body shook.

"Yes, but why? How? I don't understand." Kristen looked up as tears streamed down her face. "He was a welder and a businessman. Why would someone kill him? He did so much for us. He was like a father."

"Mrs. Hobbs, we don't have those answers at this time. The county detectives and the City of Lakewood are looking into it," the coroner said. "Does your uncle have any other family?"

"No, just me and my husband, who's out of the country on business. His wife passed away years ago of cancer. They never had children. My husband was like a son to him." Kristen turned back toward the body on the metal table and shook her head. "This just can't be … he was such a good man. How?"

As soon as she got into her car, Kristen dialed Jared's number. When Jared picked up the phone, she began to cry uncontrollably.

"Jared…" She hesitated, trying to gain her composure. "The authorities found your uncle." The line went silent for almost a minute as Kristen tried to control her crying. "He's dead."

"Dead?" Jared tried his best to act surprised.

"Jared, he's dead," she sobbed. "He was killed. I just had to identify him at the county coroner's office."

"Make sure you ask for several copies of the death certificate."

"What?" Kristen asked.

"Ah, did they say how he was killed?" Jared quickly asked, hoping to change the subject so that Kristen wouldn't question his request for more death certificates.

"They said he was strangled and his body dumped like someone's trash."

"Kristen, there's an extra set of keys to his house and shop in my top dresser drawer."

"Keys? What do I need with keys to his house and shop?"

"The police will probably need them for their investigation." Jared wanted the police to find the things he had planted in the house and shop – the things that belonged to Dustin Rodney.

"Oh, okay." Kristen was still shaken.

"Kristen, he told me he didn't want a service if anything ever happened to him. Just have a funeral home pick up his body and have it cremated. We can spread his ashes on his property once I get back."

As the word "property" rolled off his tongue, Jared thought about how much he would get for his uncle's property, beyond what the life insurance would pay.

"Jared, aren't you coming back? Don't you want to see your uncle before they ..."

"No. I want to remember him the way I saw him last." Jared thought about his uncle right before he'd taken his life – the questions his uncle had asked about McCord and the surprise on his face

when he'd realized that his own life was about
to end.

Jared told himself to focus; he had to keep
thinking about the task at hand.

"Listen, I was about to go into a meeting. I'll call
you later," Jared said.

"But Jared, you should be here."

The line went dead between them.

After Kristen had positively identified Jared's
uncle, the county detective, Jamie Kraft, dropped by
and talked to her. Kristen had mentioned having
keys to the uncle's home and shop, which Jamie
requested from her. After he finished up his
interview with Kristen, Jamie headed over to the
welding shop and home.

Jared and Mia had decided to stay in. They placed
an order for a large pizza and ate while watching
TV. After all the hours she'd put in at work, Mia was
tired, so the two cuddled on the couch while they
ate their pizza and Jared drank a beer.

When a news segment about his uncle came on,
Jared sat up. The newscaster informed the viewers
that the authorities had arrested Dustin Rodney in
connection with this murder. They were looking into
other murders in the surrounding area.

"I don't understand people like that. How can
they be so heartless? Mia asked.

"I know," Jared agreed, watching her out of the corner of his eye.

Outside of Mia's house sat Brady Coulter, PI. He had been trailing James all day. Not once had the man gone home. He'd parked his car in a hotel parking lot. After a few hours, he'd left and gone to a print shop. The BMW had been rented under the name of James Arthur Lincoln. However, when Brady ran the name "James Arthur Lincoln," he didn't find any matches. Brady tried to run a credit check, which he was allowed to do as part of a background check. Nothing matched James' age or description.

Brady found only one person: a Lakewood man in his sixties who had been a victim of identity theft several months earlier. When Brady had first talked to Dr. Al Gordon, he had thought it was just a case of an overprotective father. However, the more hours he spent on the case, the more he was beginning to believe that the man who was engaged to Mia Gordon wasn't the person he claimed to be.

The following day, Brady followed the man claiming to be James back to the hotel. While the man was inside, Brady walked over to the BMW. It was locked, so Brady looked in the windows. Nothing seemed out of the ordinary. He was checking the driver-side window when James walked over to the car.

"Can I help you with something?" James asked.

"No, just admiring the Beamer. Always wanted one," Brady responded.

James looked over the man standing by the driver-side door. He pulled out the key fob.

"They're nice cars; always had one," James said.

"This a rental or your own?" Brady asked.

"My own," James said. He pushed his way into the car. "I wouldn't be hanging around the parking lot if I were you. Security is pretty heavy here and they have cameras everywhere."

"Sure, man."

Brady knew the car was a rental, as he'd run the plate. He turned back, circled around the parking lot, and went into the café attached to the hotel. He didn't want James to see the car he was driving. Once James had pulled out of the parking lot, Brady went back to his car, then put on a baseball cap and sunglasses. The road that led out of the hotel parking lot was one-way, so he easily caught sight of the BMW and stayed a safe distance from the car. James stopped his vehicle a few office buildings down from Smiles Dental and slumped in his seat. Brady did the same.

At 3:30, Mia came out of the dental office, dressed in yoga pants and a tank top. She drove southbound. James followed her car until she pulled into Zen Yoga. He pulled his BMW into the strip mall and slumped down once again. It was clear to Brady that this man was stalking Mia … but why? What was he up to?

CHAPTER 32

Al Gordon and Brady Colter met over coffee at a local coffee shop. Using his index finger, Brady pushed the typed report to Dr. Gordon's side of the table.

"I'm still working on this, so it isn't conclusive. However, there are a few things I want you to see and, more so, be aware of," Brady said.

Dr. Gordon scanned the first paragraph, then stopped and looked up.

"He's been following my daughter?" he said, sounding more outraged with each word.

Brady said nothing. He allowed Al to vent.

"What kind of sick son of a ..." Al stopped talking when the lady at the table across from them cleared her throat disapprovingly and gave him a harsh look.

Dr. Gordon lowered his head and finished reading the report in front of him.

"Doesn't he go to work? Why would he be following her? Am I to understand that you're unable to find a James Arthur Lincoln who matches his story?" Dr. Gordon rapidly fired off questions, a confused look on his face.

"That's correct. Thus far, I've not been able to find out who this man really is. As for going to work, I can only assume that if he's tailing your daughter's every move, he doesn't have a job. I need to find a Social Security Number and a DOB for James," Brady said

Dr. Gordon sat in the booth, thinking. Then he looked back at the report. "The car is a rental as well? He told Mia he purchased the car for cash."

"Al, I can assure you, the car is a rental. I know that for certain. I ran the plate in the hopes that if the car did belong to James, I'd be able to get his DOB."

"Who is this man? What's he attempting to do with my daughter?"

"I'm not sure. All I can tell you is that he follows her any time they're not together. Has your daughter said anything about this to you? Maybe having seen him?"

"No. I assume she has no idea he's doing this. I can go back tonight and have a talk with her about what you found."

"I wouldn't do that just yet. We simply don't know enough about this guy. If you confront her now, my fear is that you'll drive her away from you and into his life even more. Have they set a wedding date yet?"

"No. Not to my knowledge, anyway. What if I talk to him myself and ask him a few questions?"

"If you can wait, I think it's best. I'll be tailing his every move."

Connor, Kate, and Sundae went out to the uncle's house on Longview Drive to meet with Detective Jamie Kraft. Detective Kraft was showing them around when Sundae began her own search. Once they were inside the shop, she kept going over to the south wall of the building. There, she'd sit and howl, signaling that she'd found something. Each time Kate and Connor walked over, they couldn't see anything.

Connor turned to go back to Detective Kraft, then returned to the wall. After a moment, he walked back to Kraft and Kate. "I'd like to request that the Lakewood Police Department bring some luminol to the shop and see if they can find anything. That is, if it's okay with the Natick County Sherriff's Department."

Forensic investigators used luminol to detect trace amounts of blood at crime scenes. Detective Kraft had no problem with that, so Kate called their CSI team to the scene.

Connor, Kate, and Sundae drove back to the

city while they waited for the results of the luminol testing. As they neared the city, Kate looked over at Connor.

"So, what are you two doing for dinner?" she asked.

Connor glanced at her and shrugged his shoulders. "Not a thing. Probably a PB and J again."

"Head over to Second Street. They just opened a new Italian restaurant. I want to try it. I'll buy," Kate said.

As Connor drove toward Second Street, Kate called in a takeout order.

"It should be ready by the time we get there," Kate said. "Do you want to eat at my place or yours?"

They decided to eat at Connor's, as it was closer and the food wouldn't get cold. Sundae's nose was in overdrive with the wonderful aroma of the food, but she settled for her bowl of kibble.

Connor walked over to an oak cabinet with a stack of stereo equipment, sitting in a corner of the living room. He turned the tuner to a country western station and set the volume on low. He then walked over to an oak wine rack and selected a bottle of Merlot.

"Is that the wine rack you made?" Kate asked, admiring the workmanship.

"Yep. Made it from oak flat board. The inlay is bloodwood," Connor said.

He walked back into the kitchen, grabbed two

wine glasses, opened the Merlot, and poured each of them a glass. Kate and Connor ate at his small table.

After dinner, they moved to the sofa and set the bottle between them on the coffee table They sat sipping wine and listening to the soft music while talking until well after midnight.

Connor looked over at Kate. Her eyes were closed; she had fallen asleep. He turned down the covers on his bed before carrying her into his bedroom. As he covered up Kate, Sundae looked at him, confused, as her bed was in his bedroom.

Connor went out to sleep in his recliner. Sundae ran back and forth until Connor grabbed her bed and put it next to his chair, where she cuddled up and fell asleep.

The following morning, Connor fried eggs and bacon. He was buttering toast when the smell of freshly cooked breakfast woke up Kate. She came out to the kitchen, rubbing sleep from her eyes.

"Good morning, Sunshine," Connor said, looking at Kate. "I have eggs, bacon, and toast." He motioned Kate to the table and they ate breakfast together.

"A girl could get used to this, you know," Kate said.

Just then, a sound alerted Connor to a text. He pulled his phone from his pocket and read it. Kate knew they had the day off, so she wondered whether he'd received the results of the luminol spray.

"That was Theresa. She's helping me find a beagle for Carlos. She has a beagle now that needs a good home," Connor said.

"That's wonderful! Carlos will be so excited."

"Only one problem. Theresa wants to make a home visit next week before placing the beagle," Connor said.

"I guess I don't see the problem…"

"They need a fenced yard. Theresa is very selective about who she'll allow to adopt her beagles. A fence is for the beagle's well-being, so he or she won't get out in traffic."

"Oh, I see."

"Want to help me build a fence today?"

"Sure, if you take me home and let me get a shower and brush my teeth first."

"That can be arranged." Connor smiled at Kate. "Oh, I almost forgot. Eric texted me early this morning. The luminol worked. They found blood splatters on the wall as well as the concrete floor. They're checking now to see if it matches any of our victims."

CHAPTER 33

C onnor and Kate looked over the CSI team's report. The team had been able to find small traces of blood. Now came the daunting task of waiting to see if their collections were actually useful and, if so, whether they could match the trace samples of blood to the victims. Sometimes, the cleaning agents a person used in an attempt to clean up the area made them useless.

The most important thing to Connor was that Sundae had alerted them to that area. He knew that the man Sundae had chased through the cemetery on the day of Amber Howell's funeral, the same man who'd knocked her out and left her for dead in an alley, had been in that very spot in that shop.

Kate broke Connor's train of thought. "Do you know that Candy Martin is reporting that the Lakewood Police have their man in custody?"

"Then why does my gut tell me that Dustin

Rodney isn't the guy? I agree he's a dirtbag but I just don't believe he's the man who killed those people."

"Connor, for once just relax. You've been putting in hour after hour on this case. Now let's go meet Theresa for the home visit at Carlos' house."

"Tell me, why is it that Sundae alerted us to blood spatter we couldn't see, yet she couldn't care less when she's in a room with Dustin?" Connor asked as he put on his sport coat.

Kate couldn't dismiss what Connor had said. She had to admit that the same thought had crossed her mind. Nonetheless, the killing had stopped once Dustin had been taken into custody. Or, at least she hoped it had. In the recesses of her mind, she worried that they simply hadn't found the next victim.

Theresa pulled up to the curb. Carlos excitedly burst out of the front door, followed by Sundae, Connor, Kate, and his grandmother. Theresa gave Connor a hug, then bent down and scratched Sundae behind the ears.

"How are you doing, little lady? Keeping Connor in line, I hope." Theresa stood and opened the passenger-side door of the van. She brought out a leashed, thirteen-inch, tri-colored female beagle.

Carlos kneeled and the little beagle ran over to

him. Theresa checked the house and the backyard fence, which Connor had paid for and which he and Kate had installed. With Carlos' help, Theresa made a list of things they needed to get for the beagle. She had Carlos and his grandmother sign a contract stating that if they no longer wanted the little beagle, they would surrender her to Theresa and not take her to a shelter. This was a contract Theresa made every new owner sign.

Connor, Kate, Carlos, Sundae, and the new beagle, whose name was now Pebbles, headed off to the pet store with the list. Once there, Connor set up and paid for a recurring food and treat service that would deliver to Carlos' house. He knew that Carlos' grandmother didn't have a car, nor did she drive, so this would remove the burden of getting the proper food for Pebbles each month. Next, Connor paid for one-on-one obedience classes for Carlos and Pebbles. The trainer would go to the house three times a week to help train Pebbles. The trainer would also teach Carlos how to be a responsible dog owner.

Carlos picked out a brand-new leash and a matching collar. Connor took the first delivery of food and treats back to the house with them. The two beagles surrounded Carlos in the backseat. Kate and Connor glanced over the seat several times as they drove Carlos and Pebbles home. In their harsh world of so much bad, the sight of this little boy's happiness made them both feel that there just might be hope, at least for this little boy.

Brady had followed the BMW driven by James to a yoga studio. However, for some reason, after the class, the BMW turned left when Mia's car made a right turn.

"What?" Brady said out loud, puzzled. This was completely out of character for the man who called himself James. Brady continued to follow the BMW while James made several other turns, leaving Mia far behind them both.

"What is this guy doing?" Brady murmured as he watched the BMW in front of him. Brady continued to tail James as he took an exit onto Highway 10. When they neared the edge of the Lakewood city limits, the BMW exited onto a frontage road. Brady backed off a little, not wanting to alert James to the fact that he was being followed.

Five miles off Highway 10, the BMW made a right turn onto a dirt road. Now theirs were the only cars on this road and clouds of dust rose up behind each of them. On Longview Drive, the BMW turned up a long driveway that led to a large country house. Brady continued on down the dirt road past the driveway.

Jared stepped out of the BMW; no one was around. He saw the dust rise up over a small dirt hill from the car that had been following him. Suddenly, the dust cloud stopped. He watched to see if the dust cloud came back in his direction. It did not.

He popped the trunk of his car and retrieved a pair of latex gloves, a tire iron, and the bottle of ether he'd taken from Smiles. He walked off toward the tree line that surrounded his uncle's property. He waited and watched his car. From this vantage point, he could see if the car came back down the road toward the BMW or the house.

Brady figured that Jared had seen him. He turned on the location finder on the extra phone whose number only Dr. Gordon had. Brady then sent Dr. Gordon a text message. He told him that James had probably seen Brady following him. He also gave the doctor a general location of where he thought he was. Brady opened his car door, tossed the phone on the floor, and pushed it under the front seat. Lastly, he grabbed an empty gas can from the back of the car. If James did happen to see him, Brady could say that he was out of gas and needed help. James might fall for that.

Brady locked the car and looked around. There didn't appear to be a house for miles, except for the one at which the BMW had turned. Slowly, Brady walked back down the dirt road. As he approached the driveway, he noticed the BMW parked right where he'd seen it pull in. He waited, watching the house and driveway. There was no movement other than a light breeze blowing through the trees that lined the property. Maybe James did own a home. This was certainly an impressive place with a lot of land.

Slowly, Brady approached the BMW. He looked through the window. No one was inside the car. He had turned to walk up to the front door when he felt something strike him from behind. Then everything went black.

CHAPTER 34

Dr. Gordon had just finished up with his last patient of the day. He noticed Mia looking upset at the front desk.

"Everything okay?" he asked.

"Just waiting for James to call or show up. We were going out and he was supposed to call after work so we could make plans," Mia said.

Dr. Gordon thought to himself, 'What work? The guy probably fell asleep in his car somewhere out front.'

"Did you call him?"

"Yes, but his phone goes right to voice mail. He didn't call while I was at my yoga class, did he?"

Dr. Gordon wondered whether he could possibly be lucky enough to have the man just move on and leave his daughter alone.

"No one called for you while you were gone. How about dinner with your dad tonight?"

Mia didn't answer, so he walked to the back room to check the machine that cleaned their instruments.

"Sure, let's go, Dad," Mia said. "James can always join us if he calls later."

Dr. Gordon silently hoped that the man wouldn't call his daughter ever again.

He locked up his office and the two of them left for dinner. Mia and the doctor had a wonderful evening out. Dr. Gordon thought it was almost like before James had set foot in his office and into Mia's life. Once again, he found himself laughing and chatting with his daughter.

Jared reattached the eyebolts to the shop wall while Brady was still unconscious. He then hoisted Brady's limp body against the wall and attached the restraints to his wrists. Once Brady was secured to the wall, Jared searched Brady's pockets and removed his keys. Locking the shop, he got into the BMW and drove down the dirt road to Brady's car.

Jared unlocked the car and searched through it. He found nothing that would explain why this man had followed him all the way through the city and out into the country. He was certain the man had followed him there. He did have a gas can in his hand, so Jared started the car up. The gas gauge showed half a tank. Jared realized that the gas can was simply a ploy to come to Jared's door, but why? Jared relocked the car, then bent down and let the air out of one of the front tires. He knew that if the sheriff's department came by, they would see a flat tire and assume the person had left the car by the side of the road to go for help.

Back at his uncle's shop, Jared sat at the desk and looked through the man's wallet. Thirty dollars in bills along with two credit cards, a debit card, and a handful of photos … but nothing at all that explained who Brady Coulter was and why he had followed him. His cell phone was locked and Jared couldn't figure out how to unlock it. He had missed a date with Mia but figured he could make up some story as to why he hadn't called or picked her up.

Finally, in the early morning hours, Brady slowly began to stir. His eyes were blurry and his shoulders hurt from holding most of his weight. Where the hell was he? He looked around and thought he was in some type of shop. He blinked but his vision was still blurry. What was the smell? It was faint but he knew he recognized it. He had a raging headache and the back of his head hurt so badly, he was having trouble remembering anything. He straightened his legs, which took the weight off his shoulders, and pressed his body weight against the wall.

The rattling of chains woke Jared. He stood up and walked over to Brady.

"You've been following me. Care to tell me why?" Jared asked sternly.

Brady looked at the man standing in front of him. He looked familiar. Brady blinked his eyes several times in an attempt to clear his vision. Who was this man and why was he – Brady – chained to a wall in a shop? Brady then remembered the photos back in his office, the case he was working on for Dr. Gordon. He was facing the man who called himself James Arthur Lincoln, the man Brady had been hired to look into.

"Look, I ran out of gas. I was simply looking for help," Brady said.

"Try again. I checked your car and you have half a tank."

"You're wrong. That gas gauge has been out for months. The thing started to sputter, so I assumed it was out of gas."

"I started it up just fine. Now tell me why you followed me."

Brady rattled the restraints, trying to free himself. Jared laughed at him.

"They've held bigger men than you, my friend."

Brady searched his mind. What was this guy talking about?

"What are you, some sicko?" Brady asked.

Jared laughed and went to the far end of the building. Brady could tell that he was looking for something.

"How long have I been here?" Brady asked.

"Let's see. You seemed to have fallen asleep yesterday afternoon."

"Yesterday?" Brady asked in disbelief.

He remembered he'd left the location finder on his phone and a brief location in his last text to Dr. Gordon. Surely, if Gordon couldn't reach him, he'd be worried and think to contact the police. Or had James found the other cell phone under the seat on the passenger side of the car?

Jared walked back in front of Brady with a small chair and sat down.

"Okay, let's start with who you are," Jared said, though he already knew.

"My name is Brady Coulter."

"Very good." Jared smiled at Brady. "Now, why were you following me, Brady?

Brady thought for a minute but couldn't think of anything. He said nothing.

Jared got up and retrieved a cattle prod from the other side of the shop. "Now, we're going to have a man-to-man talk here. I want answers. Do you understand what this is?"

Brady looked at the two-foot object in the man's hands. "No, I don't," he replied.

"This, Brady, my friend, is what they call a cattle prod. Cattlemen use it to get cattle to do what they want them to do. Only, cattle have very thick hides. You do not." Jared smiled wickedly. "Now, why were you following me?"

Brady looked down at the cattle prod.

"Tell me!" Jared screamed.

Brady said nothing. Jared approached him and pressed the prod into his chest. The voltage sent a shock through Brady's body. The shock made Brady's head hurt even more than it had before. In fact, his head was throbbing so badly, he felt like he would be sick to his stomach.

"Once again, why were you following me?"

As Jared approached, Brady used the strength in his arms to lift his weight upward. He used his legs to kick Jared firmly in the gut. The blow caught Jared off guard and knocked the breath out of him. He fell backward and hit his head on the concrete floor.

Dr. Gordon was on his way to a conference. He'd gone through security, then grabbed a latte before taking a seat at the gate. Out of his briefcase, he pulled the phone that Brady had given him so that they could stay in contact without Mia's knowledge. He noticed that the phone had lost its charge. Fumbling, he found the charger at the bottom of his briefcase. He saw an area where people were charging their phones, but no outlet was available. He should have charged the phone last night, but he was so excited that he and his daughter had reconnected that he'd totally forgotten. He had to let Brady know that he would be out of town for the night.

Finally, a teenager got up, plugged in his earphones, and unplugged his phone from the charger. Dr. Gordon quickly took his place at one of the tall stools and plugged in the phone. The phone chirped once and a partial message from Brady showed up on the screen. Quickly, Dr. Gordon scrolled to read the entire message that Brady had sent the prior afternoon:

Dr. Gordon, there's a very good possibility that James saw me following him. We left Mia's yoga class and he didn't follow her. I followed him. My car is parked on a dirt road about 15 miles off of Highway 10. I have my location finder on. If for some reason I run into trouble with this man, please contact the authorities. James pulled into a large house off this road. I will enter on foot. Thank you, Brady

Dr. Gordon looked at his watch. Brady's message had been sent hours ago. There was no follow-up message. Dr. Gordon was in the process of calling Brady's phone when he heard the announcement to board his flight. Brady's number rang until it went into voice mail. Dr. Gordon looked at his watch again. He was worried that something had happened. It wasn't like Brady to not follow up.

"Last call for Flight 1028, now boarding at Gate 10."

CHAPTER 35

D r. Gordon jumped up from the stool. He grabbed his briefcase with one hand and the extra cell phone with the other. In his haste, he forgot to unplug the phone from the charging port. A teenage boy with almost every inch of his body covered in tats called out to him.

"Hey, mister, your charger." The boy unplugged the charger and ran after Dr. Gordon.

Dr. Gordon ran toward the escalators. He had to catch a cab back to his office. The teenager caught up with him just as he was about to step on the escalator. He tapped Dr. Gordon on the shoulder.

"Hey, mister ... your charger ... you left this back there."

Dr. Gordon grabbed the charger from the kid's hand, then continued on downstairs to ground transportation

"You're welcome," the teenager muttered.

Once outside, Dr. Gordon hailed a cab. He quickly gave the cabbie the address to his dental office in Lakewood, then dialed the Natick Sherriff's Department. After several transfers, he was able to relay the information about the location that his PI had given him. Fortunately, the last person he'd spoken to actually knew Brady Coulter and took down the information along with the number of Brady's phone.

The cabbie pulled into the driveway at Smiles Dental. Dr. Gordon pulled out his debit card and handed it to the driver. The driver attached a small credit card reader to his phone and swiped the card. Dr. Gordon waited as the cabbie repeated the process three more times.

"I'm sorry, sir, but your card has been declined."

"Declined," Dr. Gordon repeated with a confused look on his face. "That's impossible. Try this one." Dr. Gordon handed another debit card to the cabbie and took back the other card. "This one is for my business."

Once again, the cabbie swiped the card several times. "I'm sorry, but this one has been declined as well."

"Listen, just use my credit card." Dr. Gordon handed a third card to the cabbie.

The charge went through and Al signed the driver's cell phone screen with his finger. He jumped out of the cab and ran to the office door. He pulled on the door, but it was locked. Dr. Gordon looked at the time. This shouldn't be … did Mia sleep in? He dropped his things onto the sidewalk and fished his keys out of his pocket. His cell phone rang just as he unlocked the front door.

"Dr. Gordon, my name is Detective Jamie Kraft with the Natick Sherriff's Department. You called about a Brady Coulter, whom you hired as a PI?"

"Yes, sir, I did. He sent me a text message yesterday afternoon, although I didn't see it until today. He hasn't followed up since that message. I've called him repeatedly and it goes into voice mail each time. Detective, I'm worried about him. It's simply not like Brady to not follow up."

"Dr. Gordon, may I ask what he was investigating for you?"

"A guy became involved with my daughter."

"I see, right." The detective sounded less interested.

"Detective, Brady found out that the name this guy gave my daughter isn't real."

"Meaning a fake name? Maybe he's married or something," Detective Kraft said.

"Look, I know I probably sound like an overprotective dad, but my daughter didn't show up for work this morning, either."

"How old is your daughter?"

Dr. Gordon rubbed his hand over his beard, frustrated with the detective.

"Detective, listen. Brady asked me to contact the authorities if I didn't hear from him. If I have to go over your head, I will. My PI is missing, as is my daughter. Now, if you would, please get off your ass and help me or I will contact the news media and the State Police. Something is very wrong. Do you understand me?"

Detective Kraft thought about this for a minute. "Dr. Gordon, do you know where Brady was last seen?"

Dr. Gordon was losing his patience. He had given this information to at least three different people at the Sherriff's Department when he'd called earlier. Nevertheless, he took the extra cell phone out of the briefcase and read the text to Detective Kraft, line for line.

Detective Kraft plugged the location into his computer using coordinates that were as close as he could get to what Dr. Gordon had given him.

"Hmm," Detective Kraft said.

"*Hmm* … What the hell does that mean?" Dr. Gordon's frustration clearly showed.

"If I'm correct, we had a crime scene in that area about a week ago. You said he left his location finder on the cell phone. Is that correct?"

"Yes."

"I'll get back to you."

"Wait, what about my daughter? I told you, she never showed up to work today."

"Dr. Gordon, are you in the county or the city?"

"City."

"Call the Lakewood Police and report her missing if you don't find that she's overslept."

Dr. Gordon hung up the phone and looked around the office for a note Mia may have left. His desk looked like someone had ransacked it while searching for something. His chair was overturned and papers were scattered around the floor. The cash drawer was empty.

Dr. Gordon felt his pulse quicken and his heart race with each passing minute. At the back of the office, he found the door open and Mia's sweater lying on the ground outside.

Dr. Gordon dialed the Lakewood Police emergency phone number.

"What's your emergency?" the dispatcher asked.

"My name is Dr. Alistair Gordon of Smiles Dental here in Lakewood. I was supposed to be at a dental conference today. Anyway, I had to come back…" The doctor was so overwhelmed, he didn't know where to start.

The well-trained dispatcher could tell this. "Take a deep breath and explain from the beginning," the dispatcher said.

Dr. Gordon talked about the text and the fact that he'd been at the airport, ready to leave, but came back to his office because he was worried. Next, he'd found his office locked when it should have been open for business, with his daughter there.

He told the dispatcher that he'd called the

Natick Sherriff's Department and reported Brady's text and lack of follow-up since yesterday. After he hung up with the Sherriff's Department, he'd found that his dental office had been ransacked and that the back door was wide open. He'd found his daughter's sweater outside the back door with what looked like a bloodstain on it. He explained why he'd hired Brady to look into this man's past and told the dispatcher that nothing the man had told his daughter so far was true.

"I'll send the detectives over right away. Are you sure no one's there now?"

"I don't think so."

"I'll stay on the line. Go check every room and closet. Dr. Gordon, please put some exam gloves on so you don't disturb any prints. Lock the front and back doors until the detectives show you an ID at your front door.

"Okay."

As he went room by room, Dr. Gordon noticed – and reported to the dispatcher – that a cabinet where he kept ether was open and that all the ether had been removed.

The dispatcher had already dispatched Connor and Kate to the location.

"Dr. Gordon, the detectives' ETA is about ten minutes. Detectives Connor Maxwell and Kate Stroup, along with a K9, will be there shortly, but I'll stay on the phone with you. Do not unlock that door until the detectives show their IDs. Do you understand?"

"Yes."

"I'm going to use another line to call your PI again. Do you know whom you talked to at the county?"

"I talked to three people, then a detective called me. His name was … God, I can't remember, I'm sorry. Oh, I forgot to tell you, and I think the county detective … when I got to my office and tried to pay the cab with my personal debit card, it was rejected. I then tried with the business debit card and it was also declined."

Sandy, the Lakewood dispatcher, sent a text to Kate, telling her that Dr. Gordon had also reported that when he tried to pay a taxi that morning with his personal and business debit cards, both had been declined. He stated that they shouldn't have been.

"PD, 15 and 49 are 10-6 at Smiles Dental," Connor radioed in.

"10-4, 15 and 49. Dr. Gordon, the detectives should be at your front door."

"They are. Thank you so much."

"My pleasure, Dr. Gordon. I hope everything is okay."

Connor held his ID and badge up to the door glass. Dr. Gordon allowed Connor, Kate, and Sundae in. Sundae quickly moved past all of them. Her tail went up and she began to howl as she inspected several places. Dr. Gordon jumped the first time she howled.

"It's him again." Connor looked over at Kate. "Go outside. Notify Barton and Harris. Dr. Gordon, what person with the county did you last talk with?"

"I talked to three people. Then a detective called me back. I thought he said his name was James, but I'm probably thinking of this guy."

The doctor pulled some photos from his briefcase and showed them to the detectives. Kate and Connor stared at them. The man's hair was now red, no longer a dark brown. He had a red beard as well. Something about his face had changed … maybe his nose? They were uncertain about what was different. What they were sure of was that the man who'd killed both Amber Howell and Garrett McCord had been here in this office. Sundae had confirmed their suspicions. Kate quickly took a snapshot of the photos and texted it to Detectives Barton and Harris and the Lakewood Police Department.

"Dr. Gordon, I have two detectives who will escort you to a safe house. Their names are Bob Barton and Grant Harris. Once we leave, relock this door and don't open it until they come to get you."

"But…" Dr. Gordon said, confused.

"We're heading out to the location your PI gave."

"I don't understand…"

"Dr. Gordon, we have to get going. Please wait for the detectives to arrive and pick you up."

With that, Connor, Kate, and Sundae left.

"PD, 15."

"Go ahead, 15."

"15 and 49 en route to Longview Drive. Please notify Detective Jamie Kraft of Natick Sherriff's Department and send him the photos Kate just sent over. Also, send out a BOLO of the photos from the doctor along with the license plate photo. It should be on a BMW."

Connor turned on the emergency lights and siren and weaved in and out of the city traffic until he neared the Highway 10 exit.

"Try Detective Kraft's cell phone again," Connor said to Kate as he drove.

"Went straight into voice mail," Kate reported.

"Have our dispatch find out whether they've heard anything from Jamie. Make sure they have the photos and BOLO. Also, give Sandy the location where we're heading on Longview," Connor said.

CHAPTER 36

Brady's car was found parked along the side of the road. Connor noticed that it had a flat front tire. Looking around, he saw no cars at the address on Longview. Not even Jamie's, the Natick County detective's car, could be seen. Connor pulled into the driveway and placed a call to the Natick Sheriff's Department dispatch.

"This is Detective Connor Maxwell. Have you heard from Detective Kraft?"

"Last we heard, he was at the address on Longview. I have a unit going out to do a welfare check there right now," the dispatcher said.

"I'm here and there are no cars. I'll check the house and the shop."

"Thank you."

Connor, Kate, and Sundae got out of the car. They were heading toward the house when Sundae veered off the sidewalk and headed toward the shop. Connor motioned to Kate in Sundae's direction. They noticed fresh tire tracks that led into the shop and disappeared at the large double doors.

Connor tried the double doors, then walked around to the small side door, which was also locked. He knocked but no one answered. With that, Connor pushed on the door. When it refused to open, he went to his car and got a heavy battering ram, which he used to open the door. He drew his Glock and stepped in, then backed out just as quickly.

"Sundae, come!" Connor commanded. Sundae ran outside. He picked up the little beagle and put her in Kate's arms. "Take her and put her in the car. There's an engine running and this place is full of carbon monoxide. Call it in."

Connor pulled his shirt up around his face and entered. Once inside, he found Jamie's unmarked car in park, with the engine running. Quickly, he turned off the car. He ran outside for another breath of fresh air.

"Jamie's car was in there, running."

"Is anyone in there?" Kate asked

"I don't know yet. Just stay out here. If I don't come out, come in and get me." Connor reentered the large shop.

He quickly opened the large doors, took another deep breath, and went back inside. He pulled his shirt up over his nose and used his flashlight instead of turning on any lights. Connor found Jamie still alive but passed out. He was cuffed to a metal machine. Using his handcuff key, Connor unlocked the cuffs. He then carried Jamie outside and laid him on the ground. "We need an ambulance ASAP!" he shouted to Kate, who was already calling it in.

Connor went back inside and found a man chained with cuffs to the wall. Connor quickly uncuffed the man, carried him outside, and laid him next to Jamie.

"This guy has a weak heartbeat," Connor said.

He went back inside once again to look for Dr. Gordon's daughter but came out for the last time with no one else. Connor staggered over to the two men and sat down, gasping for breath.

"No one else is in there," he panted.

About the time the ambulance arrived, Jamie was coming to. Connor knelt over him.

"Hey, buddy, it's Connor. I found you sucking on your tailpipe in there."

"He hit me from behind with something. When I came to, the shop was dark and my engine was running. The next thing I can remember was everything getting blurry before it all went black … I need to let my dispatch know." Jamie tried to get up but fell back down.

"Hey, you're not going anywhere for a while. Besides, Kate already told them we found you."

The EMTs were checking over Brady and loading him into the ambulance.

Jamie, did you get a look at the guy?"

"No, I'm sorry."

"Do you know if he had a young woman with him?" Connor asked.

"No. As I said, I walked in from the driveway and got clobbered over the head. When I came to, I was cuffed to a damn hunk of metal in that shop."

"15, PD," Connor said to dispatch.

"Go ahead, 15."

"I know that the owner of this property on Longview was killed. We were out here last week with Jamie. They got keys from a niece or nephew. Can you have County get in touch with whoever it was and have a unit bring them here to the property ASAP?"

"Will try," Sandy said. "Jamie okay? How about you three?"

"Jamie is doing pretty good. I'm not sure about the PI. If he wakes up, let me know so we can question him."

"15, what about the doctor's daughter?"

"Negative, not a trace."

"15, I did a background on the daughter. I'll be sending photos of her to you. She's clean, no arrests, straight-A student in high school and college.

"Thanks."

"By the way, Barton and Harris are on their way to your location."

"10-4."

The ambulance left with Jamie and Brady.

Several minutes later, Detectives Barton and Harris rolled up to the scene. Kate filled them in on what she knew as Connor looked around the property for clues. Just as he reached Barton's unmarked car, a marked county unit rolled up.

The officer let a young woman out of the car and said," This lady has the keys to the property."

Connor introduced himself and asked for her name. Kate took down everything the woman told them. She said her name was Kristen Hobbs. Her husband's uncle had owned this place for as long as she knew. Her husband, Jared Hobbs, was out of the country. The last time he'd called, he'd said he was in London.

Connor pulled a file from the dash of his car. He opened it on the hood of the county unit.

"Would you by any chance know who this man is?" Connor opened the file for James Arthur Lincoln to the first photo.

Kristen took a deep breath and stood back. "It looks like my husband, but Jared has dark brown hair. Is he okay?"

Connor turned the page to a photo of Jared and Mia in an embrace.

"I think so, Mrs. Hobbs," Connor said. He watched Kristen Hobbs take in this new information.

"Who's that woman he's with?"

"She's a missing person who we're looking for."

"Mrs. Hobbs, your husband became engaged to this woman several weeks ago," Kate said.

"Engaged. He couldn't have. He's married to me."

Connor asked, "Mrs. Hobbs, does your husband make frequent trips during which he leaves you? And what is it you said he does?"

Kate left the group and called in the ID of the person they were looking for. She asked dispatch to get any information they could on a Jared Allen Hobbs.

Connor stepped away and asked Barton and Harris to take Mrs. Hobbs in for further questioning at the Lakewood Police Department. They were to call him and Kate with any new information they received. As Mrs. Hobbs was put into the police unit, Connor heard her ask if she was under arrest and whether she needed an attorney.

Once back in their unit, Kate looked over to Connor. "How can she be married to this monster and never know anything about what he does or where he is? You can bet if I was married, my husband would be telling me what he did and where he was going."

"Copy that!" Connor said.

He called for a wrecker to pick up Brady Coulter's car so that it wasn't left on the side of the road. Connor was providing the location of the PI's vehicle as he merged back onto Highway 10. The old dirt road left a cloud of dust in his wake.

They received a call. The State Police had spotted the BMW traveling eastbound on I-40. Clearly, Jared and the BMW were now out of their jurisdiction. The location Sandy had given them was at least fifteen miles from the Lakewood city limits.

"Sandy, can you put me over to the State Police frequency? Also, please advise them that he may have Dr. Gordon's daughter as a hostage."

"Give me a second."

"Go ahead, Lakewood 15. SP 214 has your BOLO in sight."

CHAPTER 37

"SP 214, be advised that we're about two minutes from your location."

"10-4, Lakewood 15. Be advised that he just got back in the car and is on the move, heading eastbound."

"SP 214, did you see a female with him?"

"Negative, Lakewood 15. No female. He got gas, used the men's room, and is on the move."

As soon as Bob Barton and Grant Harris got word that Connor and Kate were closing in on Jared Hobbs, they got into their unit and headed in that direction running code, sirens and lights flashing.

Connor finally saw the State Police unit ahead of him in the outside lane.

"SP 214, I'm right behind you."

"10-4, Lakewood 15. Should I engage the lights?"

"Not just yet, SP 214. Be advised that I don't believe he'll give up easily. Also, in the off chance he has the girl alive in the backseat or the trunk, we need to be careful," Connor said.

"10-4, Lakewood 15."

"SP 214 to dispatch, we need this frequency cleared for only the Lakewood Police Department and me," the state trooper said.

"10-4, SP 214 and Lakewood 15."

"SP 214, do we have any other units nearby in case we need back up?"

"Stand by, SP 214."

"Kate, reach into the back and get your vest on," Connor said. "After that, give me mine and please put Sundae's on her."

Kate followed his request without saying a word. After she had put on her vest, she handed Connor his own. She took the wheel from the passenger side while he put his bulletproof vest on. Then Kate reached around and put Sundae's vest on her. Once Connor saw that they were all wearing their vests, he grabbed the mic.

"SP 214, engage!"

With that, the lights and siren came on the state trooper's car. Connor did the same.

"Lakewood 15, the rabbit is on the run!" the state trooper said.

Connor sped up behind the State Police officer's car. They were now doing 110 miles per hour along I-40. Cars were moving out of their way. After several miles at speeds between 110 and 120 miles per hour, it seemed that this was not going to end soon.

Kate received a text from Barton and Harris, stating that they were right behind them. Kate turned around in her seat and saw them.

"Barton and Harris are behind us now," Kate said.

Connor looked up in his rearview mirror and saw them. "SP 214, one of our units is right behind us in an unmarked car. Can we put one of us in front of the BMW, one of us to the side, and the other in back? Or can your guys put a spike strip up ahead?"

"Lakewood 15, let's try to box him in first."

"Okay. Can your dispatch let our Lakewood 92 and 89 on this frequency?"

"Copy that, SP?" The state trooper asked his dispatch.

"10-4, SP 214, we'll allow that."

"Let Bob know he's on the frequency with SP 214," Connor said. "Tell them to put their vests on, please."

Kate texted Harris a message about the vests.

"SP 214, I'll move my car to the front position. Lakewood 92 and 89, take the side position. SP 214, take the tail. Any shots fired, I want us all back into a safe position again," Connor said.

Connor passed the State Police car and moved to the front of the BMW.

Next, Bob and Grant came alongside the BMW, while SP214 took up the rear.

"Lakewood 92, I'm slowing down. Move as close as you can.

"10-4, 15."

With vehicles closing in around him, Jared reached across the front seat and pulled out a handgun. He pointed it at Detective Harris through his window.

"15, he's armed."

"92, back off. Repeat, back off!"

Before Bob could back off, Jared fired one round into the back window of Connor and Kate's car in front of him.

"Lakewood 15, 89, and 92, all units back away. Repeat, back away. Shots fired," Connor said.

Bob quickly backed off until he was behind the state trooper's car. Connor told Kate to reach around and bring Sundae to the front of the car. Kate grabbed Sundae and put her on the floorboards of the unit.

Another shot was fired into Connor and Kate's car

"Kate, hold Sundae with your feet and grab ahold of that sissy bar. When I tell you, get down in the seat," Connor said.

"But..." Kate said

"That's an order, detective."

With that, Connor quickly moved to the lane aside of the BMW and pulled his Glock.

"Get down!" Connor yelled as he fired at the front tire but missed. He was now behind the state trooper once again.

"SP 214 to dispatch, we've had shots fired. Permission to have units ahead place a spike strip. Maybe on that bridge. There's no place for him to run."

"10-4, SP 214. Stand by.

At this point, all they could do was follow Jared. He tried once to roll down the window of the BMW and shoot backward, but the shot went off beyond all of them.

"SP 214, we have units setting up a spike strip on the bridge, as you requested."

"Please advise them that I have two, repeat, two Lakewood Police units that are unmarked cars with me. They are both silver Chargers. Each has two passengers. One has a K9 with them as well."

"10-4, SP 214. All of you, be careful out there. We do have the 28, 29 back on the car. It's registered to a rental car franchise out of California. Last serviced and rented in the Lakewood area to a James Arthur Lincoln."

"10-4."

"Copy that, Lakewood?"

"10-4, but James Arthur Lincoln is an alias. His real name is Jared Allen Hobbs," said Connor.

"Copy that, Lakewood 15," said State Police dispatch.

The State Police unit backed off as they traveled

down the interstate. When they neared the bridge, Jared must have seen all the red lights just beyond. The spike strip was right before the bridge. Jared slowed the BMW, then quickly turned into the median and crossed the highway into the westbound lane.

"That son of a…" Connor didn't finish his sentence as he maneuvered the turn across the interstate along with the state trooper and Detectives Barton and Harris.

"SP 214, that's okay. We have a second spike strip on the westbound lane about a mile up. We'll leave a few cars here and follow you all," said one of the state troopers waiting on the opposite side of the bridge.

"10-4."

Suddenly all the tires on the BMW blew. The car swerved from left to right before it flipped on its side and came to a stop. Connor pulled his unit to the side. He saw Jared climb out the driver-side window and take off.

"Kate, check the trunk for the girl. Bob, you and Grant follow us." Connor was out of his unit at a dead run. "Give chase!" he commanded Sundae.

Sundae passed Connor and quickly caught up to Jared. She grabbed his pant leg and caused him to fall.

"Police! Stop!" yelled Connor.

Jared was back on his feet when Sundae tripped him by running across his path and sinking her teeth into his other ankle. This time, Jared leveled his gun at Sundae. She jumped and sank her teeth into Jared's gun hand.

Bob, Grant, and the state troopers moved in behind Connor. They fanned out to surround Jared.

"I really wouldn't do that if I were you," Connor said, his gun pointed at Jared.

"Then get your damn dog off me," Jared whined.

"Looks like she has a score to settle with you." Connor stood over Jared and allowed Sundae to hold on a little longer before he gave a command. "Okay, release."

Sundae backed away but kept her eyes trained on the man.

Connor got out his cuffs and cuffed Jared's hands behind his back. "Jared Allen Hobbs, you're under arrest." Connor read Jared his rights and pulled him to his feet. As they walked back to the police units parked by the interstate, Sundae walked in front of them. Jared tripped and fell face-first.

"Oops. Sundae, you shouldn't walk in front of a prisoner." Connor laughed under his breath.

"Damn little dog! I should've killed you when I had the chance."

Once back at the car, Kate pulled Connor aside and told him Mia wasn't in the car.

"So, Jared, where's the girl?" Connor asked.

Jared smiled. "She's my insurance policy. I want an attorney."

The police officers all looked at each other. They knew that once a prisoner requested an attorney, they couldn't question him anymore unless in the presence of that attorney.

Bob and Grant took Jared back to the Lakewood Police Department in their car. Kate called dispatch and asked to have both Julia McCord and Maggie come in to make a positive ID. After Jared was fingerprinted and his photo taken, he was put in a holding cell.

Kate went alone to the safe house to speak to Dr. Gordon. She knew that telling him they'd caught Jared but hadn't found his daughter would be the hardest thing she'd have to do that day.

Connor discovered that Jared wasn't the only Hobbs looking for an attorney. One of the Lakewood police officers had overheard Kristen's call to her attorney. During the call, she had related what had happened with Jared and had asked to start divorce proceedings.

Maggie made a positive ID of Jared, stating that his hair color was different. Mrs. McCord did the same. Connor put in a call to the DA for a search warrant of Jared's house and a consultation for what they could offer for the return of Mia Gordon, dead or alive. The police continued to put pressure on Jared to find Mia.

CHAPTER 38

Three weeks later, Connor and Kate received the search warrant for Jared's house, bank accounts, and investments. As Connor and Kate pulled up to the house, Connor's jaw fell open.

"Can you believe this place? It's a palace, not a house. I mean, this is a damn palace!" Connor exclaimed.

"Far cry from where he's living now," Kate said.

Kristen showed them in, along with a team who gathered together Jared's computer and everything in his office.

"Mrs. Hobbs, may I ask you something? You don't have to answer if you don't want to. Is this house paid for?" Connor asked.

"Yes, Jared paid cash for it."

Connor wondered whether Jared really had done that. He hoped Kristen wouldn't be in for another rude surprise.

"You really had no idea what he was doing?" Kate asked her.

"No, I really didn't. I'll never trust anyone that much ever again." Tears streamed down Kristen's face. "Hearing about all the people and the lives he damaged and hurt … the hardest to hear was that he'd killed his own uncle."

"Mrs. Hobbs, has he ever confided in you as to what he did with Mia?" Kate asked.

"No. I wish he would. I know that poor man lost his wife and now has no idea where his daughter is, or even if she's alive. I can promise you, if he ever tells me, I'll call you," Kristen said.

Candy Martin was in her heyday. She had interviews with Jared's ex-wife and Dr. Gordon. The latter pleaded for anyone who knew the whereabouts of his daughter to please call the Lakewood Police Department.

Connor and Kate had a scheduled meeting with Jared and his attorney. In the interview room, Jared sat in his orange jumpsuit – no Rolex on his wrist and no fancy car in the parking lot. His dark roots were beginning to show.

"Detectives, my client has asked to speak to you today about the whereabouts of Mia Gordon," Attorney Dennis Mitchell said, then sat next to Jared.

"Is that true, Jared? Or are you just jerking us around?" Connor asked.

"I'll take you out there," Jared said.

"You can't just tell us where she is?" Connor asked.

"I want a deal," Jared said. "And, no, I have to show you where."

"You and your attorney know I can ask the District Attorney's office, but that decision comes from them, not us," Connor said.

Within a week, they had a signed deal stating that Jared had to show police where Mia Gordon's body was or there would be no deal at all. They transported Jared in a heavily guarded prison van. Connor, Kate, and Sundae drove behind the van while Bob Barton and Grant Harris drove in front of it. Jared's attorney's car was behind Connor and Kate.

Jared directed the driver to a desolate area. Upon being released from the van in leg chains and cuffs, he walked about a quarter of a mile. He pointed to a spot in an arroyo. Two guards with shovels began to dig as Jared's attorney sweated in his expensive three-piece suit.

After about an hour, it was evident that Mia's body wasn't there. Jared had duped them all. He was loaded back into the van and returned to his cell.

Two weeks later, Dennis Mitchell called again. He was personally sorry but his client was now expressing remorse. If the ADA would honor the same deal, Jared would show them where to find Mia's body.

Once again, the Jared parade was on. This time, the van was directed off the highway and down a dirt road for about a mile. The prison van was flanked by Connor, Kate, and Detectives Barton and Harris. This time, Dennis Mitchell, Jared's lawyer, wore a golf shirt. Jared got out of the van, walked toward a stream, and pointed. After an hour of digging, the guards found nothing.

Connor walked over to Jared, leaned over his shoulder, and whispered, "I think I'll suggest that you be put in general population back at the prison. No more cell to yourself, fancy boy. You're a piece of dirt. You've given her father enough grief. I wish they'd leave you and me out here for an hour, you coward." Connor walked away with a smile and approached Jared's attorney. "Attorney Mitchell, may I have a few minutes out here with your client?"

"No, no, I want to go back," Jared said. "I'm not feeling well."

"Oh, I bet you aren't. You know, there are a lot of people who want to meet you back there," Connor said. He got into his car and slammed the door.

EPILOGUE

It was said that each time the prison guards came to his cell, Jared worried that Connor had somehow made good on his promise to put him in with the general population.

Dr. Gordon has never given up hope that his daughter, Mia, will come home. He keeps a single candle burning continuously in a window. So far, her body has not been found.

Brady Coulter and Jamie Kraft both fully recovered from their injuries and returned to their jobs. They are the only known survivors of Jared Hobbs.

Carlos continues to do well in school and to work with his little beagle. The last time Connor checked with the trainer, he learned that Carlos had said that he and Pebbles would one day become a search-and-rescue team. Connor and Sundae visit Carlos once a week.

Julia McCord sold the ranch. Her last known address was in Colorado.

Mr. and Mrs. Howell divorced about a year after Amber's death.

On each day of Jared's trial, Kristen Hobbs was seen sitting in the last row of the courtroom.

Jared's attorney quit after the second search for Mia's body. He could no longer stomach Jared's manipulation of people.

Jared was sentenced to two life terms in prison without the possibility of parole. His legal team filed appeal.

The Lakewood Police Department still follows up on all tips that come in on the whereabouts of Mia Gordon.

As for me … well, Sundae and I find time on our days off to walk the trails and go up into the hills and mountains. I watch the white tip of Sundae's tail, which is all that I can see, as she runs through the thick brush in search of anything she can find. I pray that Sundae doesn't find anything and that Dr. Gordon is right about Mia coming home.

The department has eased up on its restrictions regarding dating co-workers. Kate and I are seeing each other on a regular basis outside of work.

On the anniversary of his first year in prison, Jared Allen Hobbs was found dead in his prison cell. His body was hanging from a bed sheet. No note was found. I pray that there's a special place in hell for people like Jared.

A MESSAGE FROM TIM

I hope you enjoyed this book; if so, please help the
author!

Book reviews are crucial. If you enjoyed reading
Deception by Timothy Glass, here are a few
things that are vital to the success of any author. To
help me, tell others about my books. Word-of-mouth
"advertising" is the most powerful marketing tool
there is. Statistics show it is better than expensive
TV commercials or full-page magazine ads. Also,
leaving an honest review is the best way to ensure I
will be able to keep writing full time. I'd greatly
appreciate it if you'd consider leaving a rating for
the book and writing a brief review. It doesn't have
to be long, a sentence or two will help and is all that
is needed. I would greatly appreciate it.

Timothy Glass

CHAPTER 40

Timothy Glass was born in Pennsylvania
but grew up in Central New Mexico.
Tim was a first responder for almost nine years to earn money to pay for college.
Tim graduated from the University of New Mexico. He later spent some time in New England and central Florida. Glass is an award-winning author, illustrator, cartoonist, and writing instructor. Tim has worked as a
ghostwriter and a story consultant. Glass started his writing career as a journalist under the pen name of C. Stewart. He has written and published more than 400 nonfiction articles nationally and
internationally for the health and fitness

industry. Glass worked as a regular contributing writer for several New York based magazines. Until the magazine's retirement in the late 1990's, Tim was a freelance journalist for It's a Wrap magazine, a New Mexico entertainment quarterly.

VISIT US ON THE WEB

Visit Tim's website at www.timglass.com. Also, don't forget to check out his beagle cartoons at http://www.timglass.com/ Cartoons/

Join Tim on his fan pages:

Facebook: https://www.facebook.com/pages/Timothy-Glass/146746625258?ref=ts

Twitter: www.twitter.com/timothyglass/

LinkedIn: http://www.linkedin.com/in/ timothyglass

Check out our Sleepytown Beagles fabric and wrapping paper:

https://www.spoonflower.com/profiles/ sleepytown_beagles